THE BLUE BOAT

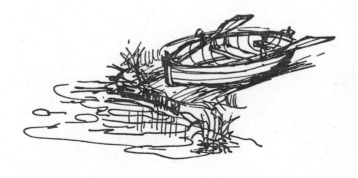

WILLIAM MAYNE

THE BLUE BOAT

Illustrated by
Geraldine Spence

NEW YORK
E. P. DUTTON & CO., INC.
1960

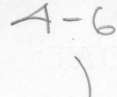

First published in the U.S.A., 1960
by E. P. Dutton & Co., Inc.

All rights reserved. Printed in the U.S.A.

Originally published and copyright, 1957, in
the United Kingdom by William Mayne.

Library of Congress Catalog Card Number: 60-6005

To J.F.B.
in exchange for
a god-daughter

Contents

I

The Bridge Station

Mrs Wrigley had told Christopher the way to the railway station. He should have gone through the town, but although the town had been fully in sight all the time, he had never found himself inside it: it had stayed over to the left and come no nearer. In fact, after some time it had vanished altogether, and Christopher was walking along a country road that seemed to have no idea of going anywhere but round its own corners. Several people had passed, and he had wondered whether to ask

I

them the way, but it would have been foolish to ask if he would be there in a moment in any case.

The town must surely be left behind now, he thought. He went slowly round the next bend, to see what lay beyond before turning about and trying again. He saw from the bend that the road ran under the railway, which was held above it by a black iron bridge. What was more, the signal by the bridge dropped to 'Halt', and in the distance a train rumbled, and a railway station bell rang twice.

'In just good time,' said Christopher to an afternoon-sleeping cat in the bottom of a twiggy hedge. He walked quickly to the bridge, found the kissing gate called 'Way up', and went up the stepped path.

'Are you going on t'train?' said the ticket collector in the doorway, in a voice that would disbelieve if he said yes.

Christopher said 'No, I'm just meeting my brother. He's come from Africa.'

'This train's nobbut come from Town,' said the ticket-collector. 'Happen though it's met them that's come out of Africa.'

'He came by aeroplane,' said Christopher.

'I dessay they've let him on and never minded,' said the ticket-collector. 'They aren't particular about folk.'

'His name's Hugh,' said Christopher: since the man wanted to talk he might as well be told what was wanted.

'Here she comes,' said the ticket-collector. 'It'll be interesting to see a black lad.'

'Oh, he isn't black,' said Christopher. 'Only sunburnt, I expect.'

'What's black but that,' said the ticket-collector. 'They get black I know on t'sands in Withern, and it's nearer t'sun in Africa.'

The train slowed itself into the station. The engine stopped beside Christopher and stood like a lump of noisy black heat. The fireman came down to talk to the ticket-collector. No passenger got off the train. The only doors to open were those in the luggage van, and out of there the porter and the guard brought a wheelbarrow, and a box called 'Higget, Withern Bridge'.

Christopher waited, but no one else even peered from the carriage windows. The fireman finished his talk (about pigs) with the ticket collector, and climbed up into his fire-place of a room, and made the engine sing a softer hissing note.

'Is he none here?' said the ticket-collector to Christopher.

'He hasn't got off,' said Christopher. 'He mightn't know how to get off.'

'More like he hasn't known to get on,' said the ticket-collector. 'No railways, I dessay.' He went to the cab of the engine, and said: 'Frank, have you brought a black man with you?'

'I'm the blackest in the train,' said Frank, the fireman.

'I mean a born African black,' said the ticket-collector.

'He isn't,' said Christopher. 'He's white, like anybody else.'

'Anybody but Frank,' said the ticket collector. 'I'll look along t'train, and you can look with me.'

They did not look far. In the first compartment, next to the engine Hugh sat, looking out at the other side of the track.

'Hugh,' said Christopher. 'You get out here.'

'Oh, hello,' said Hugh, looking round for a moment. 'I don't. I get out at the next station.' Then he went back to looking out of the window with his usual air of not caring what Christopher's opinion was, because it was bound to be wrong. He was much bigger now than he was when Christopher last saw him, and his air of being right was very convincing.

'But I've come to meet you,' said Christopher, because he had come to the station, and here was Hugh.

'Not here,' said Hugh.

'Well now,' said the ticket-collector, 'the train's bound on. Let's see your ticket, you African.'

'Here it is,' said Hugh, and brought out the little green card.

'Aye,' said the ticket-collector. 'It's right enough: you're to go on to Withern.'

Hugh nodded, because he had known all the time.

'You've come to t'wrong station,' said the ticket-collector to Christopher. 'This is Withern Bridge. You'd better both stop in t'train while it takes you to Withern. It's fourpence single—I'll fetch you t'ticket.'

Christopher gave him fourpence, and went to sit opposite Hugh.

'I was just looking out of the window,' said Hugh. 'At the sea. Have you been swimming yet?'

4

'Mrs Wrigley said it was too cold,' said Christopher. 'So I haven't looked at the sea or the beach.'

'Not much beach,' said Hugh.

Christopher looked with him at the water, where it showed a mile away between trees.

'Islands, too,' said Hugh. 'With little trees on them.'

'Perhaps the tide's come up high,' said Christopher. 'There might be more beach when it's low.'

The ticket-collector came to the carriage with Christopher's fourpenny ticket. Hugh was saying 'There aren't any tides in Africa.'

'No tides down there, neither,' said the ticket-collector. 'That's nobbut t'Mere. T'sea's on my side. Well, don't forget to get yourselves off: you won't get no farther if you stop on at t'next station—it's t'last.' He banged the door shut, gave the fireman a nod, and went back to his office. The train moved itself out of the station, and rattled itself along an embankment through the fields, as soon as it had ground its hollow way over the iron bridge.

Ahead and to the left lay the town of Withern. Beyond the town and the station, and reaching across the landscape into the right-hand horizon there was the sea. The train ran downhill, and the nearer it came to the sea the less they saw of the water and the more they saw of the land, until they came under the station roof at Withern, and saw only those brick walls.

'Now you can meet me,' said Hugh. 'Mother and Dad send their love.'

'What was it like in the aeroplane?' said Christopher.

'All right,' said Hugh. 'What's it like in England, being at school all the time? Do you have lessons all day?'

'Nearly all day,' said Christopher. 'Hadn't we better get out?'

Hugh said: 'Nobody's opened the door yet.'

'You have to do it yourself,' said Christopher. 'Don't you do things in Africa?'

'A boy does it,' said Hugh. 'A black man.' He opened the carriage door and jumped out.

'Not that side,' said Christopher. 'There's a platform to get out on to.'

But Hugh had not stayed to see whether he was right or not. He had walked to the engine and climbed up into the cab with Frank and the driver.

Christopher got out on the lawful side, and went to see what Hugh was doing. He almost fell over the uncoupling rod that was being used to loose the engine from its carriages.

'Careful then,' said the man to him, and 'Right away', to the engine. The engine moved away, with Hugh aboard, without the train.

'Are you coming or going?' said the man with the rod.

'Going,' said Christopher. Then he remembered that you always go from a station whether by train or by just walking out. 'At least, we've come on the train and we're going away from the station in a car.'

'Well, have you any bags?' said the man.

Christopher thought Hugh might have some luggage with him, because although aeroplanes will not bring any,

6

there were a good many things belonging to him still in England, without any home to keep them in.

Christopher and the man looked in the compartment and found a bag and a mackintosh, and the man pointed out how illegal and dangerous it was to get out on the wrong side of the train, particularly if you left the door open. Christopher explained that only two days ago Hugh had still been in Africa.

'Brought the sunshine with him,' said the man. They left the bag and the mackintosh on the platform and went to the back of the train to look in the luggage compartment.

Whilst they walked along, the engine, which had gone beyond the station, over a level crossing, had a set of points changed for it and crossed the road again, came back on the next line. It went beyond the station again, drank at the elephant trunk of the water tower, crossed more points, and came frontways on to the carriages, so that the train changed ends; and by the time Christopher and the man had come to the front of the train, it was no more the front but the back.

There were two boxes that belonged to Hugh. The man first linked the engine to the carriages, then put his stick away and brought out the boxes. Hugh came down from the engine cab with a black-freckled face.

'I drove down,' he said.

'It's against the rules,' said Christopher. 'Have you any more luggage, Hugh?' He said nothing of his envy of the ride in the engine: it was little use ever saying anything about Hugh's luckiness in everything, even in being taken to Africa by boat, and living there with Mother and Dad, and coming back by air. It is not fair, they said, to complain about someone else's luck. Nor perhaps, was it fair to congratulate them on it, because luck is no one's fault or excellence.

Hugh had no more luggage, he thought. The man changed his occupation entirely from coupler to porter, and wheeled the two boxes to the station gate. Hugh stayed a moment and had a word with Frank, the fireman, and then joined Christopher, who was with the boxes.

Mr Wrigley drove up in the car. Christopher wondered what would be said about Hugh's appearance. 'The man at the other station thought you were going to be black,' he said.

'Stupid,' said Hugh.

'You are black now,' said Christopher. 'Anyway, this is Mr Wrigley coming, where we've got to stay.'

'I'd rather be at home,' said Hugh: he meant in Africa.

'Hush,' said Christopher. 'He says we have to make ourselves at home.'

'At whose home?' said Hugh.

II

Nobody at Home

HUGH was the same oakish brown all over. He showed
Christopher when they shared the bath that evening.
'I'm the exact colour of the floor,' he said. 'You're the
exact colour of the bath.'

'It was a very bad winter,' said Christopher, trying to
make a well-borne hardship equal Hugh's good fortune.
'There was no sunshine for a long time.'

'I like snow,' said Hugh, regretting his missed winters.
'But I like hot too. But the bath water isn't very hot tonight.'

'It never is,' said Christopher, 'In fact, I think it's a
beastly place, this house.'

Hugh found the tablet of round pink soap and tried to
balance it on his wet brown knees. 'It makes them shine
pink as well,' he said, looking at the reflection. 'But it
would be all right here, because of Mrs Wrigley being
Mother's friend, wouldn't it?'

'It's like school,' said Christopher. 'You mustn't touch
things, or walk on the grass, or sing in bed.'

'I'm going to, though,' said Hugh, sliding the soap down
his shins. 'Mother doesn't mind, so Mrs Wrigley couldn't.'

'She could,' said Christopher. 'Easily. But when's
Mother and Dad coming here?'

'They aren't,' said Hugh. 'Dad said he was going to look

9

for somewhere to live, and if he found a nice place he
might stay in England.'

'A real house for us all,' said Christopher. 'I wish he
would: I hate staying at school in the holidays, and I hate
coming here.'

'It's all right at home in Africa,' said Hugh. 'We've got
a house there.'

'But I've never been to it or seen it,' said Christopher. 'You are wearing away the soap, Hugh.'

Hugh put the soap back on the rack between him and Christopher, and said, 'I'm not going to wash in this cold water, so I washed the soap instead to make it look as if I had.'

Christopher agreed with him, so they let the chilly water run away and went to bed. Mrs Wrigley came to look at them and the shape filled the doorway for a moment: she was very large without being at all fat. She said 'Good night, boys,' in a deep voice, turned out the light, and closed the door.

'Nobody's kissed me,' said Hugh.

'Nor me, for a long time,' said Christopher. 'You get used to it.'

In the morning, after breakfast, there was a whole wide empty day to consider. Hugh thought about it whilst his mouth was still full of marmalade, and got up from the table to look out of the window.

Mrs Wrigley, behind the teapot, reminded him that he had not finished.

'Oh, I have, nearly,' said Hugh, and went on looking at the place outside. 'What shall we do today, Christopher?' he said.

'You can go down on the sands,' said Mrs Wrigley. 'It's a warm day, but you can't go in the sea yet. Christopher knows the way to the front: you can go there this morning.'

'I've never been there,' said Christopher.

'It's just below the station,' said Mrs Wrigley. 'You went there yesterday.'

'Yes,' said Christopher: they had neither of them explained the roundabout road he had taken.

Hugh, in the window behind Mrs Wrigley, was laying his finger across his lips for silence, and pointing with his other hand to Mrs Wrigley's cat, which was called Soot.

Mr Wrigley said Soot to rhyme with 'boot', and Mrs Wrigley said Soot to rhyme with 'but'. Hugh had some idea about the cat. When Christopher had finished he went with Hugh into the garden.

'Don't walk on the grass,' said Mrs Wrigley, and closed the door on them.

'What did I tell you?' said Christopher.

'Well, it's very dangerous,' said Hugh.

'Why?' said Christopher. 'There aren't any scorpions or snakes.'

'I wasn't thinking about the grass,' said Hugh. 'I was thinking of Mrs Wrigley and her cat. She's a witch, I should think.'

'A witch doctor,' said Christopher, wondering what Hugh might have seen of such men in Africa.

'No, an ordinary witch,' said Hugh. 'You can't tell them from ordinary people except by their black cat.'

'There's a black cat at school,' said Christopher. 'It's called Tiny because it's too big to sleep on a chair.'

'Somebody there is a witch,' said Hugh. 'It's a rule.'

'The headmaster's mother is,' said Christopher. 'But what can witches do?'

'I don't know,' said Hugh. 'But it explains why they're like that.'

'Mother's friends aren't witches,' said Christopher.

'Witches can make you to be their friends. She might want to eat us,' said Hugh.

Christopher thought this was an interesting game, even if Hugh had invented it. Whilst Hugh was thinking of a way of escaping being eaten Christopher invented one without thinking at all. 'I shall carry a piece of wood about,' he said. 'So that if she wants to feel how fat my fingers are she'll think I'm thin.'

'We'll make a whole hand each,' said Hugh. 'All out of wood.'

'Not out of garden wood,' said Christopher. 'She wouldn't let us do that.'

They went out of the garden into the road, and sat under Mrs Wrigley's hedge, to be out of sight whilst they decided where to go.

Christopher knew that to the left the road went down to the main Withern road, and to the right led to a village four miles away, and then to another six miles away: he had read the signpost.

'I don't want to go along a road,' said Hugh, when he knew where they went. 'It's all roads in Africa.'

'Roads go to places,' said Christopher. 'You can always get back. I only got lost yesterday because none of the signposts said Withern on them, because I was really in Withern all the time.'

'We don't want to go anywhere she knows,' said Hugh. 'Let's go into that field, and up that hill, and there's some trees there to make wooden hands out of. And I'm going to call it The Beach, so we can say we've been there when we really came here. We could make a fire.'

Christopher was hardly willing to leave the road and cross the field, because going anywhere without orders or permission seemed risky: even holidays spent at school were full of regulation. 'Trespassing,' he said, to give a reason for obeying his unwillingness.

'We're not doing anything against the queen,' said Hugh. 'No, that's treason, isn't it?'

'Nobody said we could go,' said Christopher. 'And I have to keep you in order because you're younger, or I shall get into trouble.'

'I'll run away from you,' said Hugh, and skipped

across the road, climbed the gate, and started up the field.

Christopher followed him, and got left farther and farther behind: Hugh went up the hill like a wheel, and was ratting in the top hedge for a gap when Christopher caught him.

'Push,' said Hugh, and Christopher pushed. Hugh went through the thicketty hedge into the wood, tumbled on his knees down a sandy cliff among the tree roots, and was sitting covered in gravel and twigs and grass, brown like a hedge root: well disguised in fact; and in a sprouting elder bush.

Christopher came through more carefully on his hands as well as his knees, and stayed at the top of the little pit Hugh had fallen into.

Hugh looked round and said: 'Come down here, Christopher. Don't stand up: just crawl.'

Christopher crawled down, until he was with Hugh in the elder bush, leaning against the stiff smooth stalks.

'It's like a hammock,' said Hugh, swinging himself backwards and being pushed up again by the bush. 'But, you see, where are we?'

'You said you would call it The Beach,' said Christopher.

'We will,' said Hugh. 'But where are we going now?'

'To make a wooden hand,' said Christopher.

'Never mind about that,' said Hugh. 'We're exploring somewhere, and I didn't know where, or who we could be.'

'Maligan at the Cape of Horn,' said Christopher, bringing out some name of history.

16

'Never heard of him,' said Hugh. 'Do you think it might be the moon? Perhaps we've been caught by a man-eating flower. I can feel it closing in to a bite.'

They thought about the biting flower, and felt it drawing itself tighter round them, and had to get up out of it.

'Brush yourself,' said Christopher. 'Oughtn't we to go back?'

'Can't,' said Hugh. 'No rocket fuel. We shall have to find some atoms. Anyway, I'm not on the moon now at all. I want to be going somewhere like America, to live in.'

'So do I,' said Christopher. 'But really I do, as well as exploring places.'

'I know,' said Hugh. 'It's just England, because that's really the place we want to stay. We could call it East England, or something. New England.'

'There's already a place called New England,' said Christopher. 'It's in America. But won't England do, just England?'

'Old England would be better,' said Hugh. 'Nobody would call anywhere else Old England: you only call places New or East or North.'

'A new place, though,' said Christopher.

'Quite new,' said Hugh. 'Nobody could have known of it by map. We'll build a house in it.'

'And a garden,' said Christopher; but Hugh had never had a garden to look after, and did not mind about it; all it meant to him was not walking on the grass, though grass is quite meant for it.

17

'There's a whole fortnight,' said Hugh. 'Then they'll come for us. They might have a house too.'

'I wish they would,' said Christopher. 'What if we found a good place for one: they might make one in the place we found.'

'They might,' said Hugh. 'Dad likes new places.'

'We could try to find a really good place,' said Christopher, 'and tell them we want to live there. That's two against two.'

'I wouldn't mind where,' said Hugh. 'I want to be with them always.'

'So do I,' said Christopher. 'But you get used to it.'

III

The Sunk Road

HUGH would have led on deeper into the wood, but Christopher was troubled at leaving Mrs Wrigley without word of where they were.

'It doesn't matter,' said Hugh. 'We're having a holiday, not a school.'

Christopher climbed up the little cliff and looked down the field through the hedge. Mrs Wrigley's head—all that he could see of her—was moving among the mole hills, looking from side to side. Then she called for them by name.

'She's rising out of the ground,' said Christopher. 'She'll catch us.'

'I don't mind being caught,' said Hugh. 'But I don't want her to find our place.'

Christopher's opinion was different entirely: he cared

nothing for the place and everything about being caught.

'This way,' said Hugh. 'We don't want the witch to get us.'

'I forgot she was a witch,' said Christopher. He did not think it quite fair to call people in authority witches so that you could defy them without doing wrong. But he followed Hugh along the little cliff behind the hedge, until they passed the place where another hedge joined it on the field side; and then Hugh got through on to the fields again.

'You are a mess,' said Christopher. 'You wait until she sees you.'

'I know what to do,' said Hugh, and banged himself on the nose with the back of his hand, and started to sob with his throat at the same time. 'I'll cry,' he said, and he was crying already, 'because I fell over. You can have helped me,' and he held on to Christopher like an unsteady cripple, and edged his way down the hill to the road.

Mrs Wrigley met them there, and Hugh snuffled and sobbed and rubbed his knees, so that he was led into the kitchen and given a boiled sweet that tasted of tin. Christopher had one as well, because Hugh had held his hand in such a trusting way. Hugh was not so pleased with his acting when it led Mrs Wrigley to wash his knees and iodine them; but after it all he thought he knew how to handle Mrs Wrigley. He had forgotten for the moment that she was a witch.

'You mustn't go up there,' said Mrs Wrigley. 'It's private property, as well as being a scrapy old place full of thorns.'

'I'm better now,' said Hugh, because he had run out of tears and sobs.

'Do you think you can walk down to the sands?' said Mrs Wrigley. 'With your cut knee?'

'I'm better,' said Hugh again.

'You don't want sand in it again,' said Mrs Wrigley. 'You'd better sit in the garden this morning where I can see you.'

'I'd rather go on to the beach,' said Hugh; but he lost the fight, and Mrs Wrigley put him in the garden with a deck chair so that she could see him, and put Christopher to weeding a flower bed: he had said he liked gardening.

'That was jolly good,' said Christopher. 'It saved a lot of trouble.'

'She witched my thoughts and revenged herself,' said Hugh. 'I don't want to sit here.'

'You invented being hurt,' said Christopher. 'I wish celandines weren't so pretty, because you have to throw them away.'

Hugh kicked his heels on the path, which was what the deck chair stood on, and said one or two words in an African language, now that he knew no one would understand them.

By dinner time he was in a great silent fury, but Christopher had enjoyed himself in the safe weeding, and was happy. He found that anything dangerous and slightly against the rules was very upsetting and made him frightened. Hugh never felt unsafe at all.

After dinner, which Hugh made faces about when Mrs

Wrigley wasn't looking, but which Christopher thought better than school dinner, they were sent off to the beach. Hugh dodged back into the woodlands as soon as they came to a concealing hedge, and broke through, at a different place from this morning, but on top of the same sandy small cliff.

'Carefully,' said Christopher. Hugh climbed down like a newly washed mountaineer keeping clean. They stood among the trees and their roots, finding out that where they were was not a pit, but a long trench below the crest of the hill.

'We can go along here like anything,' said Hugh. 'This is an old road.'

'Indians,' said Christopher.

'Not a road in America,' said Hugh. 'It's just an old road in a forest, and we don't know where it leads.'

'Not to the beach,' said Christopher, wishing that it did lead where they were sent.

'Come on,' said Hugh. 'She's a witch.'

He led the way along the sunken road. It curved to the left all the time, and fell lower and lower as it went, until they came out of it and out of the wood at the same moment; or they would have done if Hugh had not stopped and looked back, and refused to go out of the shadows until he had thoroughly worked the woodland up into a magic forest.

'Nobody has ever been here,' he said. 'Not for a hundred years. It's not like an African jungle: it's much more dangerous. There aren't any animals, you see: it's too dangerous for them; and the trees don't grow, and if you speak you might be caught by a creature; and if you eat you might turn into a tree yourself. All those trees are people.'

'No they aren't,' said Christopher, not liking the idea in the least: it was too much like one of those dreams that came when he slept alone in the dormitory during the holidays, with the pale glare of the skylight the only visible thing when he woke and knew that the beds and lockers round him were alive.

'They're sure to frighten you,' said Hugh. 'Trees do anyway.'

'Let's go on,' said Christopher. 'It's clear out there.'

'But more dangerous,' said Hugh. 'I'll tell you why.' He thought for a moment. 'It's another world,' he said. 'If you go there you might get changed into things you've never heard of.'

'What are they like at all?'

'I don't know,' said Hugh. 'How could I?'

Christopher thought he could well have not mentioned it in the beginning. 'Well, go on,' he said.

'I daren't,' said Hugh. 'What if there was something there?'

'What if there's something here?' said Christopher.

'It's worse out there,' said Hugh; but Christopher pushed him and they left the woodland together.

They came out on to a place of green grass with trees round three sides, and on the fourth side the water of a lake; and on the lake were islands, and round the lake was the same hillside forest they had passed through. At the far end of the lake there was a little town smoke, and the only sounds came from the invisible birds in the trees.

'This is another land,' said Hugh. 'Shall we go away?'

'Never,' said Christopher. 'Let's build a house in this field.'

'Do you want to?' said Hugh. 'There's water getting into my feet under the grass. Quicksands, I expect. Do you think I'm sinking up to my neck?'

'You might,' said Christopher. 'Come out at once.'

'Don't pull yet,' said Hugh. 'Oh, yes do: I'm going down.'

Christopher pulled him out, not sure whether Hugh was busily thinking himself into sinking, or whether he really was being dragged down.

'We can't go across there,' said Hugh.

'What's Mrs Wrigley going to say about your sandals?' said Christopher.

Hugh replied with two African words, and they went back to the edge of the wood and sat on a fallen grey branch whilst Hugh took off his sandals and began to scrape them clean with grass and last year's leaves.

'She'll never think we've been on the beach,' said Christopher. 'We don't even know where it is.'

'Why do you have such a sad life?' said Hugh, picking himself another pad of cleaning grass. 'She's a witch, and it would be terrible to obey her when she's not there. You have to when she is.'

'You make everything sound like a sort of war,' said

Christopher. 'Her being a witch, and this wood being dead people.'

'Not dead, only changed,' said Hugh.

'Then this place is being dangerous too,' said Christopher.

'We wouldn't come here if they weren't,' said Hugh. 'Dad and I don't go to easy places.' He put on his right sandal and took off his left. 'We can go and look for sea servants,' he said. 'There ought to be some bad ones here.'

'Sea serpents,' said Christopher. 'Snake things.'

'We were very lucky to reach land at all,' said Hugh. 'First we've got to find fresh water and then build a fire in case a ship passes. That was the worst storm in living memory.'

'What are you now?' said Christopher.

Hugh put his sandal on again and became a plain shipwrecked sailor. Christopher thought he would be a plain inhabitant of the land, but Hugh would not let him because he knew so little of the country. He had to be a fellow sailor.

'I only want to be a sailor because I haven't thought about how to go on in the dangerous magic place,' said Hugh. 'We can explore the wood this side, and drink in the lake.'

'Not drink: it might be bad water,' said Christopher.

'It's salt sea water,' said Hugh. 'I nearly forgot.'

So they went back into the lower part of the wood, and it was an ordinary wood with English aconite and English daffodils; and they walked round the margin of the lake until they came to a fence among the trees, and when they had followed the fence up the hill it ran against the road, and when they had climbed through with their discoveries of flowers they walked back to the house the road side of the hedges, and came to Mrs Wrigley at tea time; who thought little of their wild flowers and sent them to wash whilst she softened the margarine.

IV

Sand in the Shoes

Mrs Wrigley gave them a newspaper to spread out and undress on. 'I don't want sand all over the house,' she said. 'And when you've got it on the paper leave it on and don't whisk about near it.'

'We didn't get very sandy,' said Hugh: there was a difficulty here if they were expected to drip sand when they had been nowhere near it.

'You do as I tell you and never mind what you think,' said Mrs Wrigley. 'It won't hurt you to stand on the newspaper.'

They stood on the newspaper, and left on it three dead leaves, a twig, a moth's wing that Hugh found on purpose, and one small pebble from an empty space in Christopher's sandal.

'She won't think much of that,' said Hugh, but Mrs Wrigley said, 'You see what a mess it saves,' and took the paper up.

'We'll get some sand tomorrow,' said Hugh. 'Then she'll never think we've been to another land and not her seaside.'

In the morning Hugh borrowed a small sack that had held garden stuff. He got it from Mr Wrigley, who was looking in the garden before breakfast. Hugh rolled the bag up and put it deep into his pocket. It was a white cloth

bag, labelled 'Chemical Fertilizer', so rolling it up did not destroy its strength. Mr Wrigley said nothing about it, and went off to catch his bus to Town.

'Can we go to the beach again?' Hugh asked. 'We found a good place, didn't we, Christopher?'

'I didn't like it much,' said Christopher, because if he said 'Yes' that was a lie.

'I'm sure two boys ought to be happy on a beach,' said Mrs Wrigley, who was slightly offended that Christopher might not be entirely pleased to do what she suggested.

'He always grumbles,' said Hugh.

'Your mother wouldn't like to hear you complaining,' said Mrs Wrigley.

'She hasn't heard me do anything for a long time,' said Christopher, 'and I like weeding the garden better.'

'You'll like it after a bit down there,' said Mrs Wrigley. 'Everybody does.' She was satisfied then, because she would rather have people share her opinions than obey her.

Hugh went down to the beach this morning. Christopher was pleased to see him obediently walking into Withern. They found the way readily, because there were signposts saying 'To the beach' at each corner where there might have been any doubt. It was a long dull walk, after they had left the borders of the woodland. There was one glimpse of the lake, with a notice that said 'Private Fishing', and then the walls of the town houses closed the road on either hand. There was only one shop on the way, and they bought nothing there in case there was a better shop soon. But even when they reached the sea there were no shops.

To get to the beach they went down fifty concrete steps in a concrete wall, across a concrete path, and down a concrete slope on to the trampled sand. The sand was twenty feet wide, and beyond that the muddy surf licked at the footprints on the land.

'It sounds all right,' said Hugh. 'It's nice sand, isn't it?'

'Look what they did to the cliffs,' said Christopher. 'They must have killed hundreds of flowers and lizards.'

'It's like a dam,' said Hugh. The whole front of the town

had been cased in concrete, as far as they could see on either hand, except in the far distance where the land jutted out in proper wild cliff.

'No rocks,' said Christopher. 'No rock pools.'

'No boats,' said Hugh. 'No people. Only us. I'm glad we haven't come here.'

'We have,' said Christopher.

'Not for long,' said Hugh. He brought the bag from his pocket and began to fill it with sand. Christopher held the mouth of the bag open until Hugh thought it was full enough and humped it up into his arms. He did not speak until he was at the top of the fifty steps that led up the concrete cliff.

'That was one end of the world,' he said. 'We're the only people there since it began, and all those footprints belong to the people who went away as soon as they could. Of course, nobody must speak down there.'

'We did,' said Christopher.

'Hush,' said Hugh. 'Not us. We've got our witch powder, let's go away at once and buy some sweets in that shop.'

The sand was a dragging load, and twice before they reached the sweet shop they had had to sit down on the bag and rest. Hugh once wanted to leave some in a gateway, but Christopher would not let him abandon his load.

'Witch powder is pretty heavy,' said Hugh. 'Always. Sometimes it's so heavy they can't carry it away, and then they never get rid of the witch.'

'Is it to get rid of her?' said Christopher. He did not

want to enter into any private magic with Hugh: let those that live on it meddle with spells, he thought.

'This isn't the heaviest, I said,' said Hugh. 'This is only to make her think something different. We'll put it on the newspaper at night. I should think we've got enough for a fortnight.'

The sweet shop had a good selection of pennyworths, and even halfpennyworths of Ogo Pogo's eyes.

'You can't eat African pennyworths,' said Hugh. 'And the English things are sixpence, and they don't have anything like this that you can buy.'

The rest of the journey passed in a dribbling silence, and they unable to say a word to each other until they came to the place where wood met road and they could go under the fence, take out the Ogo Pogo's eyes, and rest their legs and jaws.

'I like my cheeks puffed out,' said Christopher.

'Mine have forgotten,' said Hugh. 'They can't stretch: that's why I've dribbled more than you.'

The explored end of the sunk road, with the trees that had once been people, was hard to find, but they struck it after a combing search and started along it.

'I wish we knew who each person was,' said Hugh, when they rested again under a beech tree. 'This tree's got a face on it, you see, and I expect someone would know him.'

'It might be a her,' said Christopher. 'Trees are both.'

'These are all men,' said Hugh. 'Explorers trying to find their way round. But it must be the wrong way, or they wouldn't have been changed so, would they?'

31

'Why can we go along it?' said Christopher, trying to destroy Hugh's arguments before they could frighten either of them.

'Because,' said Hugh, 'because we aren't going to where this road leads. It must go to some place."

'We've been to the other end,' said Christopher. 'And that was safe, wasn't it?'

'No,' said Hugh. 'We must have a rule not to walk all the way along it. We'd better go out of it now in case we forget.'

The wood was in front of them when they climbed the side of the sunk road, and beyond the wood, shining through the trees, was the lake. They had stood at the end of it yesterday, when they had come on it for the first time, not counting the quick look they had had from the train. Christopher remembered that short sight of water, and what the ticket collector had called it.

'This is the Mere,' he said. 'Withern Mere: I heard Mr Wrigley say something about it one day. A mere is a lake.'

'Lakes are usually called lake something,' said Hugh.

'This is the Mere,' said Christopher, hoping that the common ordinary name would leave Hugh without any reason for making it magic or haunted.

'Mere,' said Hugh. 'Mere. It doesn't matter what it's called: it's still about the same to think about, and pretty dangerous.'

Then he thought it was Christopher's turn for the bag of sand, and being free ran down ahead to the water's edge.

The Mere had its own small sand cliff that stood a foot high in little bights and bays, and sometimes vanished for a few yards, leaving the edge of the water a damp tangle of reed roots that grew drier and drier until there was land with grass and then trees. Sometimes too the water ran back into the trees so that the roots made breakwaters and harbours and little havens for the trees' own seaborne fallen leaves.

They left the sand on a dry knoll where a mole had worked, and walked over water among the lake-lapped roots until Hugh tired of the game and sat kicking a cave into a little cliff and tumbling the pebbles into the still water, breaking the reflections of the bare overhead branches.

'You see,' said Hugh, 'it isn't only this side of the lake.'

'The Mere,' said Christopher.

'They want to get to the other side,' said Hugh. 'Or they used to. I don't expect anyone's tried for a long time, because they don't seem to bother about it, do they? But they do magic in Africa, because the boys told me sometimes.'

'What did they do?' said Christopher. 'It wasn't true, anyway, because magic doesn't work.'

'They say it does,' said Hugh. 'Look at all the witches we know.'

'Mrs Wrigley is the only one,' said Christopher. 'And you only said so. Besides, what does it do?'

'You get gold, or cows,' said Hugh. 'Cows in Africa, when you've magicked your neighbour away, and gold in

33

England, when you've magicked your way to the right place.'

Christopher thought about that until he saw a fish under a ridge in the bottom of the Mere, and put his mind to thinking of that, so it was Hugh who answered himself. 'But perhaps they never looked this side,' he said. 'It would be a pity if we didn't and there was some ready for us.'

'It would be safer than going along those trees,' said Christopher: when he was away from the sunk road he felt no dread of it; but Hugh's insistence on its horrors convinced him when he was there.

'It would be much safer,' said Hugh. 'I think we ought to look where we are now. We've got a bag to put it all in, and we could give a bit to Mrs Wrigley and keep her quiet.'

'Come on,' said Christopher, 'let's look at once.' He wanted to find something real and actual, something that Hugh could not turn into anything else. But Hugh had another idea to put him down with.

'Of course, we'll have to be careful,' he said. 'They may not turn us into trees, but they might not like us to take their gold. They may do something to us.'

'Who are they?' said Christopher. 'Who are they this time?'

'I don't know,' said Hugh. 'I'll think of them before we start.'

V

A Waterhill

HUGH began to think of what kind of creature it was
that guarded the gold of the Mere. He went into a
deep thought about it, gazing into the Mere in silence.
Christopher stood beside a tree and listened to a wood-
louse eating in a dead branch. It made more noise than a
snail, he thought; but there might be more than one wood-
louse there.

Hugh leapt up, having thought his thoughts and having
frightened himself out of staying in the wood. Though his
fear was of nothing he could tell about, Christopher
shared it too, and they ran up the slope from the edge of
the water, over the ridges of the sunk road, and out
through the hedge into the open fields.

'What were they?' said Christopher: all Hugh had said

was, 'They only take hold of you. No, there's only one of them,' and that had been enough to startle his feet into running.

'I still don't know what it could be,' said Hugh. 'I was just frightened of it.'

'You've left the bag of sand in there,' said Christopher. 'Right at the bottom of the hill by the water.'

'That's gold dust,' said Hugh. 'They were coming to get us when we had to run away: they wanted their gold back.'

'I'll go and get it,' said Christopher, who was perfectly happy in woods, and thought them friendly—when Hugh was not there to panic him.

'Good-bye, old friend,' said Hugh, being an explorer's companion for the time being.

Christopher left him staring out an imaginary lion that threatened the camp, and ran down through the wood to the bag of sand, and coming up the hill not so fast this time, because of the weight, and wondering about woodpeckers, and, when his feet kicked an anthill, anteaters—woodpeckers eat ants but anteaters are more interesting in shape.

Hugh had finished with the lion, and was scrambling in the hedge destroying troops that deployed in the wood, keeping the path safe and clear for Christopher, who was greeted by Hugh hearing the National Anthem and sending a telegram to the Queen for gallantry.

'Well done,' he said. 'We were starving.' The gold dust was biscuits now.

Christopher was timekeeper, because he had the unbreakable waterproof watch that never needed winding or taking off his wrist. The time was twelve o'clock, and there was an hour in which to get back to Mrs Wrigley's. They used it up in walking the five fields to the house. Hugh named them Egypt, Libya, Tunisia, Algeria and Morocco, although he found no Nile for Egypt.

'This bag of desert sand,' he said, when it was his turn for it, 'will always remind us of our own country.'

'Which country?' said Christopher, thinking for a jealous moment that Hugh meant the home he had in Africa.

'Arab's land,' said Hugh. 'That's a very thin camel you have, my friend. I am afraid I could not think of buying it. Take it away before it dies in my courtyard.'

Christopher began to think he was no good at playing any of Hugh's games. When he kept silent again, because he had nothing to say about camels, Hugh was angry and said: 'Why don't you help me? You used to before you went away.'

'You went away, not me,' said Christopher. 'And it frightens me when you pretend, so I'm not going to.'

'It frightens me too,' said Hugh. 'I like being frightened at home, but I hate it here.'

'Don't be frightened any more,' said Christopher. 'I don't like being frightened at all.'

'But I like to think of things different from what they are,' said Hugh. 'It's more interesting if you do, you see.'

'I've got used to things being proper,' said Christopher.

'You can pretend if you like, but pretend they're better.'

'I pretended gold from that sand,' said Hugh. 'And that was better, really; but it got into the worst thing I've thought of.'

'Have wishes, instead,' said Christopher. 'I wish that we hadn't finished those sweets.'

Hugh wished that his wishes would come true, and then that Mrs Wrigley would turn to paper and be blown away; but when they came out on to the road and walked to the house Mrs Wrigley was in the kitchen window holding her face out of the steam from the cooking.

Hugh forgot that the bag of sand had any secret purpose, and walked into the house with it under his arm. Mrs Wrigley only sent him on out of the kitchen to wash; and he was able to hide the sand in his smallest case under his bed.

Mrs Wrigley asked them whether they had enjoyed themselves, without mentioning the beach. They could say yes to it without being exact, and to distract Mrs Wrigley from more questions Hugh dropped a potato on the carpet: it was enough to shock Mrs Wrigley into silence, once she had scolded him.

'You can go out again afterwards,' she said, when she had become quite calm again. 'You're looking better for your holiday already, Christopher. I don't suppose they give you anything interesting in the way of food at school.'

'It's the same as this,' said Christopher; and in speaking the truth he again offended Mrs Wrigley, but she took it as kindly as she could and gladly sent them out of the way again.

'Camel,' said Hugh, when they were in the fields again. 'She-camel,' and he meant Mrs Wrigley.

'She's all right,' said Christopher. He thought Mrs Wrigley was as like school as makes no odds, without having the disadvantage that some other pupil might make her angry with all of them. His desire to be at home with the rest of the family had made him restless when Hugh was expected and when Hugh had come, but now he was back in the same position as usual: being looked after by someone who only did it from duty, not because he belonged to them; and as far as he knew life was always like that: only when Hugh first came had he been impatient of it.

'Good plump one,' said Hugh, still thinking of camels. They dropped through the hedge into the sunk road again, and went down to the shore of the lake.

'We could fish,' said Christopher, when Hugh stopped talking about what the captain of the aeroplane had said and began to decide instead that this wood was the sort of place where people might live who . . .

'We could paddle,' said Hugh. 'Or even swim. We'll paddle first because it might be too cold.'

It was at first almost too cold for paddling, but by perseverance and wriggling the toes they managed to walk about in a little bay with a sandy cliff they could sit on and a gravelly bed that was clean. When they were used to the way the water bit at their skin they went out farther, to knee depth, until they felt they were half-way out into the Mere.

When they began to come back they realized how far they had been. All at once Hugh stepped off the shallow shelf with one foot and found deep water. He had Christopher close beside him, and they swayed together when he grabbed at him to save himself. They retreated from the deep part and speculated, because it seemed to be between them and the land, and across where they had walked.

'Perhaps they put it there when we'd got past,' said Hugh, and frightened himself.

'We've come back a different way,' said Christopher. 'We'll have to feel with our feet where we want to go.'

Whilst they had stood still the ripples that walking makes in water had settled, and round their feet was stillness.

'Do you know,' said Hugh, 'there's a hill in the water over that deep part.'

'Don't be silly,' said Christopher. 'Water's flat, and you know it.'

'I don't always pretend,' said Hugh. 'Look at it.'

Hugh was using natural sense now, and Christopher could see what he reported: there was indeed a little milling hill of water where Hugh had trodden.

'It isn't hot,' said Hugh. 'But it looks boiling.'

'What makes it?' said Christopher. And they stood looking at it and listening, and they heard it running over itself, and they saw how it stood in one place and did not move.

'I don't think it's an animal,' said Hugh: now he had

something in sight he could not understand he was determined not to make a terror out of it.

'But it's got between us and the land,' said Christopher,
who felt that they were well cut off.

'Let's just walk round it,' said Hugh. 'I'm sure we came
this way.'

They edged round the mysterious swell, toe-feeling for
the deepnesses, but there were none. Once round the
watery hill the way was flat to the shore, and they came
straight to the place they had left from and found their
socks and sandals.

'I can't see that lump at all,' said Hugh. 'Do you think
it's stopped breathing?'

'I don't know what it was doing,' said Christopher.
'Don't keep making it alive: it can only be an ordinary
thing.'

'I think it was disordinary,' said Hugh. 'But my feet
have got used to the water: shall we go on walking along
the coast?'

Christopher agreed to if they kept close to the shore and
did not invent animals in the depths. Hugh agreed to keep
his fancy in order, and they coasted along the woodside.

Again it was Hugh who almost fell into the depths.
This time, though, there was no swirling hill: only the
calm Mere water gently rippled by their legs. They stood
still in their own reflections and made sure that no hill of
water rose up, and then tried to go round the deep part.
But there was no going round this deep: it stretched out
into the Mere until the water beside it was over their knees,

and it came in to the shore so close that they had to leave the water to go round the end of it, at the place where the trees ran their leggy roots out from the land, where they had found tiny harbours and havens the day before. They found the other side of the deep water, and followed that bank out into the Mere as far as they could. When their eyes were used to the water they thought they saw the other edge and even the bottom of the channel winding across the Mere bed.

'A river under the water,' said Hugh. 'For submarines to sail along.'

Then they went back to the land because their feet were trembling cold. They could not warm them in the wood, so they went into the fields again, through the one called Libya and on to the road, and when they were on the road they wanted Ogo Pogo's eyes, and walked into Withern to the only little shop they knew and bought one each and sucked them all the way home, until they came to the house and Mrs Wrigley made them spit them out and drop them into the tea-leaf tray in the sink, and the cat got blackly up to look at them.

'We can get them out later,' said Hugh, when they were alone before tea. But he was wrong. When he passed through the kitchen again they had gone, and the tea-leaves with them, and the cat lay asleep before the kitchen range, until he prodded it to see whether the precious eyes were inside. They were not, and the cat went to sleep again. Hugh would have stayed to stroke it, but he remembered it was a witch's cat and went back to Christopher.

VI

A Wish

'You can do a bit more in the garden after tea, Christopher,' said Mrs Wrigley 'Mr Wrigley will be pleased to see some weeding done, I know.'

'What about me?' said Hugh. 'I'm only good at pulling up flowers.'

'Christopher can tell you,' said Mrs Wrigley; and having given them something to do she went back to keeping the tea-pot in order.

Christopher was pleased to garden. Hugh was not pleased to do anything for Mrs Wrigley. 'Not after she's stolen my sweet and given it to the cat, he said. 'I know that's what happened to them.'

'Cats don't eat sweets,' said Christopher. 'We sometimes give them to the cat at school and it just walks away.'

'Hers ate them and then sat still,' said Hugh. 'Let's be sucking poison next time, and make it sick them up like the lions.'

'You can't suck poison,' said Christopher, and won the argument.

Hugh would not weed, and when Christopher was busily inching along the border he crept from bush to bush to the front gate and crawled out flat on his stomach, and Mr Wrigley had to step over him. Hugh expected to be turned back from the road, but Mr Wrigley was too shy to say anything to someone so very busy at crawling, and went on into the house for his tea.

Hugh gained the road, laid his ear to the ground, and decided that nothing was coming. He crawled across the road, still on his belly, being, for the moment, an alligator looking for a ditch. Then he came to the field, and began to be once more some explorer getting on in years and wishing to retire to some newly discovered place and build a house and live there with his family.

The fields were out of sunlight now, because they were on the north side of the wood and the sun was going down. The new grass was almost blue where it grew against the wood. Hugh stood and watched it darken. He decided that this was a pleasant valley, and then turned round to see whether it was a valley side or a hill side. He saw Mrs Wrigley's house below, and decided that he was only on a hill and not in a valley, and certainly not far enough away from other people to want to settle there. But it would have been pleasant to have a blue lawn, he thought.

He climbed into the wood, and wherever he came it was quiet and shadowy under the tree trunks. He stood against a tree, because he needed something behind him in the twilight.

There was a squirrel leaping against the sky, and a black quiet thing flew down to the water, and there was nothing but calm peace in the wood. Yet that was not enough: an explorer's house should have open land round it. He had seen them in Africa, in clearings, not in forests.

Though he felt no discomfort in the wood he went

straight down it to the water's edge, where one side of where he stood or walked was clear and free.

For the first time he looked across the Mere at the distant woods that closed it in. He let his eye walk round from where an island blocked the farther view, to where the nearer wood on his right closed it again, just this side of the open place at the end of the sunken road.

He saw how the sunlight fell behind the trees opposite, and shone down on to more clearings: they showed yellow behind the dark trees that fringed them and the Mere. And over there was the absolute peace of a quite unknown land where no man had walked or travelled. And the proper way to get there, he knew now, was not by land, but by water: there was Old England waiting to be discovered and dwelt in; and this side of the Mere was no magic place but the old and tired land of the present inhabitants.

'A boat,' he said. 'I wish I had a boat,' and he closed his eyes and then looked to either side; but there was no boat: a wish is no good if the land is no longer magic. As he looked and longed the sun came down in red and began to nest in the trees to the far right, and he could no longer look there, and when he had looked and made his sight black and blue he bent his head to the water. Something moved at the foot of the little cliff. Hugh stood at the top of the cliff, and whilst he watched he was the explorer at the edge of the sea, looking down a hundred feet at the beach, which for the time being was a hundred feet wide instead of fifteen inches.

The sand just under the water still moved. 'Whirlpool,' said Hugh to himself. 'Or volcano starting. Or one of those things the ship nearly sank on this afternoon,' remembering the hill in the water.

But out of the sand came something so hideous that his imagination had no need to work, and even after he had re-ordered himself so that things were their proper size the creature chilled his thoughts. It was a soaked grey in colour, wrinkled, and about five inches long—at first, of course, it seemed as big as a dragon. It had two great nipping claws at the front, and a curled-under tail, long feelers, and many legs below itself and it crawled under the water, with its back breaking and rippling the surface, until it was out of sight under the silver sheet of the sunset Mere.

Hugh waited at the top of his cliff until he thought what he should do. How many more of these monsters were there? Was that a baby and were there greater ones in the

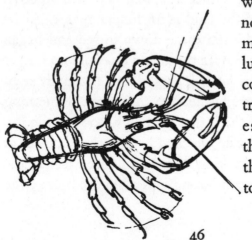

water? Had this afternoon's waterhill been made by another, lurking as big as a cow in the pit he had trodden in? Had they escaped by inches those great claws? Had those feelers not quite touched their ankles? Something touched his leg now, above his fallen sock. He jumped round, and saw only dry grass from last year daintily stroking in the wind.

He came up through the wood with his mind shut, in case it saw creatures in every tree. Until he was out in the fields again he was terrified, and when he reached the dusking grass he walked down to the bottom behind the hedge and paced about trying to calm himself.

Mrs Wrigley had come into the garden to tell Christopher that it was now too dark to weed, and that it was time for bed in any case. 'Where's Hugh?' she said. 'He hasn't gone out into the road, has he?'

'I'll go and find him,' said Christopher. 'I know where he is.' Finding Hugh should, he thought, be very simple. He left Mrs Wrigley at the gate and went across the road and into the field opposite, across the field by the hedge, slowly, waiting until Mrs Wrigley should no longer be watching. She went indoors in a moment, and Christopher went on into the wood.

It was dark there now, and the ground was doubly able to trip him up and make him stumble, but he felt with his feet all the way, and guided by the whiteness of the water, came down to the edge of the Mere. The last of the day spread itself over the water, and the sky might have been reflecting the water, or the water the sky. Hugh was not by the water. Christopher stayed for a while to see what he might see; and there was a bat over the shore and the shallows, and the black birds floating like dust over the trees near the town.

47

There was a little bubbling noise in the water below, and when he looked he saw the water move, and there was a creature eating some captured delicacy, bent over it so that what it ate was invisible. Christopher knelt to watch it more closely: he knew what the creature was, though he had not seen one before. In the shadowing water he watched a crayfish. Hugh had seen another of the same kind, and it had sent him out of the wood to pace the fields in fright. But Christopher had looked in books and read about these crayfish, and knew that they lived in water, and that people sometimes ate them as a sort of fresh-water lobster. The crayfish moved away again. Christopher would have tried to catch it, but the light was going, and he had not found Hugh.

He walked farther along the bank of the Mere, and when he came to the place where the trees stood in water he found something else, but not a natural creature this time.

It was a small, shallow, blue boat. It had been pulled up on to the shore between two trees, so that it was lying on grass and not roots. In it were two oars and a rudder. There was nobody beside it and nobody to be heard near. Christopher thought at once that this was private land with somebody's private boat, and that they had caught Hugh and taken him to Withern for some legal punishment.

That being so, and Hugh not being here, he walked up through the wood again, until he climbed through the hedge, and at the bottom of the field called Egypt, there was Hugh, waiting by the gate to see what it was that came out of the wood.

'Hello,' said Christopher, 'what's the matter? Did they catch you?'

'No,' said Hugh. 'But I saw one of them, and I didn't make them up this time. Did you see them as well?'

'No,' said Christopher. 'But I knew they'd been there. I thought they might have caught you and taken you away.'

'Please don't say things about it,' said Hugh, 'It was the dreadfullest thing I've ever seen.'

'What was?' said Christopher. Hugh had something more in his conversation than a blue boat.

'I don't want to talk about them here,' said Hugh. 'I want Mother, because she would tell me something else.'

'Tell me,' said Christopher. 'Tell me what it was.'

'It was a monster,' said Hugh. 'A monster in the water, and it crawled about.'

'Was it big?' said Christopher.

'Very small,' said Hugh. 'But very nasty. And there'll be bigger ones in the lake. It crawled near my feet. We might have trodden on one this afternoon, didn't you know?'

'Had it got great big claws?' said Christopher. 'And did it eat things?'

'Awful claws; awful feelers,' said Hugh. 'I won't go there again.'

'I saw one as well,' said Christopher. 'There's quite a lot of them, I should think, but I've never seen one before. They're crayfish, and people eat them. But I thought real people might have caught you.'

'Are they always small?' said Hugh. 'Not bigger?'

'Tiny lobsters,' said Christopher. 'But didn't you see a man?'

'No,' said Hugh. 'Only the crabfish. Then I came here, because I didn't know what it was, and things tickled my leg.'

'It wasn't anything bad,' said Christopher, and he took Hugh's hand and held it, and Hugh held it tightly back so that climbing the gate was awkward.

'Don't go back yet,' said Hugh. 'I want to cry, and I won't cry with her. I want Mother.'

They stood by the gate until Hugh had cried enough.

'I don't want to cry,' he said. 'But I do want to as well, because I want Mother.'

'You get used to it,' said Christopher. 'Are you better now?'

'Yes,' said Hugh. 'I'll say I banged my nose. It wasn't really the crabfish. Before I saw the crabfish I looked right across the Mere, and the other side looks lovely. I wished that we could go there.'

'You know where the trees are in the water,' said Christopher. 'That's why I wondered if someone had caught you on their land, because there was a boat there, with some oars.'

'A boat?' said Hugh. 'But I'd just wished for a boat when I wished to be the other side of the Mere. I wished for a boat.'

VII

The Wish

MRS WRIGLEY met them in the road, and hurried them in and to their bath. She left them and went downstairs again, angry that they were not already in bed, because they spoilt her evening quiet.

'The water's about as hot as the Mere,' said Christopher. 'I'll get in and warm it up for you.'

'I can't remember what I said when I wished for the boat,' said Hugh. 'I must have been doing something that would make things come true. Perhaps that crabfish was a fairy or something.'

'You aren't to believe in fairies now,' said Christopher. 'They would say you were too old.'

'I've got to believe in something that brings wishes when I wish them,' said Hugh. 'I know stories about them too. Do you think Mrs Wrigley is a wicked step-mother?'

'Yes,' said Christopher. 'And we never got those

wooden hands we were going to make. What if she found out?' He meant 'What if she found out we thought she was a witch?'

'It's better than being eaten,' said Hugh. 'And it's your turn to have your back to the taps.'

Hugh devoted his washing time to an experiment in making mountains out of water by squeezing his palms together under water. With a gentle squeeze he made a good hill; with a quick powerful one he spurted water out of the bath and on to the wall, where it ran down behind the bath.

'That'll fall down her neck and boil,' he said. 'Water does boil if you pour it on witches.'

'You ought to wash,' said Christopher.

'Let me be a crabfish and then I'll come out,' said Hugh. Christopher stood up and dried himself whilst Hugh nippered at his ankles until the water ran out and stranded him. Mrs Wrigley came to hurry them up. Hugh wrapped a towel round him and ran into their bedroom, to sprinkle sand on the newspaper they undressed on. Mrs Wrigley came in a little while and took the newspaper away. 'You have been enjoying yourselves,' she said.

'Yes,' said Hugh, and hid his unwashed knees as soon as possible. Mrs Wrigley put out the light and left them.

'I wish I knew what I'd done for magic,' said Hugh. 'I read a story about a boy with a magic walking stick, and he turned it round to wish; but I don't know what I did.'

'You probably didn't do anything,' said Christopher. 'It's probably someone's boat which won't be there in the morning and who'll send us out of the wood for ever; and we shall have to go on to the beach.'

'Hmn,' said Hugh, determined not to leave the wood except for the far side of the Mere. He went to sleep thinking of how he might wish; and experimenting, wishing each time that there was an Ogo Pogo's eye under the pillow, and feeling for it after each wish with less and less hope until he did not trouble to look and then he dreamt he found it and woke sadly later with his empty mouth tasting only toothpaste.

In the morning they were out as soon after breakfast as Mrs Wrigley would let them go. She stood in the sunshine herself and watched them along the road, so they did not leave it until they were at the fence that ran through the wood.

'It must still be there,' said Hugh. 'It must.'

'No reason,' said Christopher. 'I don't see why it should be at all. I think it was left there by someone who owns the land and they'll send us out or say we're stealing the boat.'

'I wished it,' said Hugh. 'And why do stories have wishes in if they're not true?'

'Why do people put boats there if they don't belong to somebody,' said Christopher. 'But I'll come with you if you go in it. I wish wishes were true.'

'They are,' said Hugh. 'You saw they were.'

To see whether the wish had remained fulfilled they stalked the place where the trees stood in water, and came nearest to it behind a thicket of bramble, and lay there without daring to look farther in case they were wrong.

Nothing moved in the wood. The stiller they lay the stiller was the silence. Only the Mere spoke above its own quietness, bubbling and lapping in the way of all still water.

'Go on,' said Hugh. 'Look.'

'You look,' said Christopher, and that invitation Hugh had been waiting for. He stood up and walked round the thicket and did not come back.

Christopher followed him. He was standing by the water under the trees looking at a small blue rowing boat that lay dry on the grass with shipped oars and unshipped rudder.

'There,' he said. 'It's quite believed, isn't it?'

'Yes,' said Christopher. 'That's where it was.'

Hugh examined his wish and found it sound in all respects, dry inside, well painted, and complete but for a name.

'I will call her the *Wish*,' he said. 'It isn't a new boat: perhaps they had to wish it from a long way off; or it might have been used before.'

'It's been used before,' said Christopher. 'It isn't a wish boat at all: it belongs to somebody else and we shall get into trouble for touching it.'

'Let's put it into the water,' said Hugh. 'No, don't yet because I haven't said thank you.' He stood on dry land again and said 'Thank you for my wish. I will only use it for good things and purposes.'

When he had finished his thanks he laid hold of the bows of the *Wish* and pulled, and the little boat slid off the land on to the tree roots, and off the tree roots into the water, and then bobbed on the Mere free and alone. Christopher stepped on the roots and picked up the dangling rope that was fastened in the bows, and held the boat: it had slid away from Hugh who had stayed in the grass.

'Get in,' said Hugh. 'You first, because it's my boat.'

'It isn't,' said Christopher. 'We shall be nearly killed with trouble about it, I know.'

'Never us,' said Hugh. 'Isn't there an anchor?'

'No,' said Christopher. 'You tie these boats up when you get to land.'

'What's that thing, then?'

'It's the rudder,' said Christopher. 'You have to pin it in the flat end, which is the back.'

'Like a hinge,' said Hugh. 'There's some things ready for it now. Give it to me.'

He knelt on the land and dropped the rudder on to its pintles and pinched a black blister on the edge of his hand, and had to dangle it in the water until the pain went from his arm. When he had recovered he got into the boat after Christopher. Christopher let go of the grass on the bank and pushed. They were free of the land.

At first they each took an oar, but there was only one pair of rowlocks and the little boat was too narrow for them to sit side by side and row, as well as steer with the cords, so Christopher climbed back to be steersman and Hugh took both oars.

He had them one at a time in the water, and the first voyage took them from where they had drifted back again to the shore, and when Christopher pushed again, the boat swung round and the rudder got off its pintles and fell into the Mere by itself. Christopher had the cords of it and pulled it aboard and dropped it back into its place. Hugh tried again, aiming for the island in the lake.

They went backwards into the bank again, because Hugh had both oars in the water for a great pull. The rudder folded against the bank and came out again and lay on the beach.

'It went backwards,' said Hugh. 'Do you think it's the steering?'

'No,' said Christopher. 'I think you rowed backwards.'

'You do have to pull,' said Hugh. 'It won't go through the water if you push.'

'I think you're doing something wrong,' said Christopher. 'Try again, but let's start so we go along the water and not into the bank.'

After half a dozen pushes had brought them forward a little way Hugh naturally pulled, and they went backwards again.

'When I get a good pull to go to a place I go away from it,' said Hugh. 'Perhaps there was something wrong with the wish.'

Christopher knew the answer now. 'You're the wrong way round,' he said. 'The rowing person faces backwards, and the other person steers. Then they can talk.'

'You do it,' said Hugh, and stood up and found the boat rocked so much that he went down on his hands as well as his feet, and camel-walked to Christopher, who camel-walked to the rowing thwart and sat down facing astern.

He pulled slowly, making sure each time that the oar blade was under water. As often as not it shot out of the water as he pulled, and the other times it dug in so much that he began to slide off the thwart into the bows of the boat.

'We're going,' said Hugh. But they had not gone far when the rudder came out of its place again and lay in the water, and the next moment the boat stuck on the bottom of the Mere and the oars touched the bottom on either side.

'The rudder won't go in again,' said Hugh, who had retrieved it and was trying to drop it on to its pintles.

'Is it broken?' said Christopher in great anxiety, because he knew that if they broke it the owner would turn up in less than a minute and cause trouble.

'The ground's in the way,' said Hugh. 'You'll have to go backwards.'

But they were stuck on sand, and Christopher had to get out and let the boat rise in the water before it would move. He pushed it back into the deeper water and got in again.

'It nearly turned over,' said Hugh, who was holding on with hands and feet.

'I know,' said Christopher, and crawled himself round on to the thwart again.

Hugh headed for the island again, and again the rudder jumped off. Christopher saw it move and stopped rowing

forwards and pushed on the oars instead, and they
grounded so lightly that they were off again without having to wade.

By the time half an hour had passed they were expert
at fending themselves off shoals, but they were only half-
way to the island, Looking at it from another way they
were only a quarter of the way there, because they had not
gone towards it at all, but only left the Mere shore.

'Your turn to row,' said Christopher. 'I want to see how

to steer. There isn't anyone on the land wanting their boat back, is there?'

'Of course not,' said Hugh, without looking. Christopher looked, but there was no one.

With Hugh rowing in a haphazard in-and-out-of-the-water manner they went at the same rate, but with only one grounding. The water grew darker below, and they seemed to come out of the shallows. By little and by little they came towards the island, and grounded again.

Christopher brought the rudder inboard and laid it in the boat. He got out again and stepped into the muddy gravel. Hugh stayed in the boat, thinking still of crayfish. Christopher laid hold of the painter and walked in the water, trying to approach the island without grounding the boat again. He found he had to keep well away until he was quarter of the way round, and on the south side there was a channel that led into the island's shore. He got in again and Hugh rowed right up and under the trees, touched the land and brought the oars into the boat and laid them along the sides. The first voyage was a success: they had come to an island.

VIII

Beaver Island

IT was easy to see, even from the creek they were in now, that there was no one on the island. But whilst they looked and waited and wondered who would be first ashore, they heard the noise of the island. It seemed like a voice at first, very shrill and talking fast; but it never stopped to breathe and no one answered it.

'Chattering,' said Hugh. 'What chatters?'

'Squirrels,' said Christopher. 'Or baby birds.'

They tied the boat to a tree and got ashore together.

'No one knows who was first,' said Hugh. 'It is a secret of exploring. This is English land now. Do you think these trees are people?'

'No. I think they're just trees,' said Christopher. 'Do different people turn into different trees? I mean, some into ash trees and some into oaks and some into horse-chestnuts?'

Hugh considered the matter. 'No,' he said. 'You change into a tree the same sort of shape: that's why all the trees in the magic road were tall good ones, because all the people who were changed were tall good people and knights. But these people were witches and step-mothers and ugly sisters, because all their trees are little and ugly.'

'What would Mrs Wrigley be?' said Christopher.

'A fat willow tree with no branches, only the hair sort

on the very top,' said Hugh. 'And Mr Wrigley would be one of those thorny trees in a hedge.'

'Hawthorn,' said Christopher. 'With white flowers.'

Even this small conversation lasted them across the island through the elders and alders and bramble, into the edging marsh and reeds. Because of the way they had come round the island to land they were facing the shore they had left, and they had to sort themselves out and rethink where they were.

'We haven't even a compass,' said Hugh. 'Most people have those: they did in the aeroplane, because the captain told me.'

'We've got the sun,' said Christopher. 'We can steer by that.'

'Oh no,' said Hugh, 'we can't. That's not the sun, it's the moon. We have to travel at night.'

'All right,' said Christopher; but he privately disagreed with pretending anything of the sort, so he went on in sunlight and Hugh went on by moonlight.

They quartered the island and thought they had seen all of it. There only remained the mountain in the middle to climb, Hugh said. It was not a great mountain: only the size of Mr Wrigley's greenhouse; and they climbed it in a moment and sat on top where there was bare rock.

The voice of the island still spoke and sounded.

'It might be starlings,' said Christopher. 'But it comes from inside the mountain.'

'Beavers,' said Hugh. 'This is Beaver Island. Those are baby beavers in the mountain.'

'I don't know what they are,' said Christopher. 'Perhaps it isn't animals at all.'

'We don't need to know everything,' said Hugh. 'Let's go on in the *Wish* again.'

And now, thought Christopher, even if it isn't our boat, we are bringing it back to land.

Hugh took the oars, and Christopher turned the *Wish* round before getting in himself. They rowed for the far shore, the unvisited one, until Christopher looked at his watch and calculated how long it might take to row back to the place they had first left. He thought they ought to go back at once, and when Hugh could not be persuaded he steered the boat in a circle and headed it towards the home port, and Hugh did not notice.

Progress was very slow, and Hugh missed more and more strokes, and once missed with both oars and banged his head on the gunwhale. After that he studied in fury the equal dipping of oars and they went even more slowly. Then they ran hard aground in a blind underwater creek and had to walk back forty feet before they found a clear channel. Christopher thought it was well time to be on the road to Mrs Wrigley's, so he got out and led the boat in by paddling alongside the deep channel, whilst Hugh rowed. Christopher held the painter and pulled at each stroke, so that good speed was made by both.

'I'm getting better at it,' said Hugh, and was too exhausted to help Christopher land the *Wish* in its grassy cradle under the trees.

'Don't sit down,' said Christopher. 'Put your shoes on

and hurry up: we're going to be late if you don't come.'

'We've got to get back,' said Hugh, prepared to consider hurrying because he thought they had crossed the lake and would have another boat journey home, and put his socks and sandals on and followed Christopher, who led the way through the wood.

'This is our side,' said Hugh, when he realized that he knew the wood. 'How did we get here?'

'I led you,' said Christopher. 'I steered. Come on, we're nearly late, and you don't want her to find out.'

'I wonder if she would be a willow tree,' said Hugh. 'Can't we wait and see? I'm sure she would change if we let her.'

They came to the gate in good time, but they needed a fair amount of washing. 'We'd better be clean,' said Christopher. 'If we aren't she'll wonder where we got the mud and she'll know it's not the beach.'

Their cleaning was not enough: Mrs Wrigley noticed a muddiness about them and said so.

'Only a little muddy,' said Hugh.

'I didn't think I should need to tell you boys that you mustn't climb about on the cliffs,' she said. 'It's not at all safe: they're always coming down into the sea. You ought to be more sensible.'

'We washed,' said Hugh. 'You know.'

'You mustn't try to deceive me,' said Mrs Wrigley. 'Never mind about the mud now: you'll have a bath tonight.'

Hugh feared they might not be let out after dinner, so

he said no more; but after dinner, when Mrs Wrigley was not there, he demonstrated to the cat that he had not been frightened. The cat fled up the curtains, and did not come when Mrs Wrigley called 'Sut, Sut, Sut, dinner, dear.' They left her looking for it, and with another last order about the cliffs went down the road.

The *Wish* was where they had left her. There was a little water in the bottom now, that had run from their feet and from the rudder and the oars. It was not enough to tip out, and they left it in, and cast off again with Christopher at the oars and Hugh steering.

'Go straight,' said Christopher to Hugh. 'If I go crooked keep the boat straight.'

They went towards the middle of the Mere, leaving the island to the right, which was the east. The rudder came off once more when they went over some shallow and pushed it off its pintles: otherwise the voyage was easy until they were near the far shore.

They grounded firmly once, and Christopher had to pilot again, walking through the water. There seemed to be a shallow edge round the Mere; but there had been a deep place on the first shore, and a deep place into the island, so there would possibly be a deep place to this shore: a deep-water channel.

'Let's drift in a magic way,' said Hugh, 'I'm sure a wish boat will take us to the right places.'

'So will a stolen boat,' said Christopher. 'If it is stolen.' But it did not feel stolen, and he got back in again to drift with Hugh.

The easiest drifting was done by poling in water just deep enough with one oar. The boat went out sideways, and drifted in again sideways, and if it was left to itself it grounded again.

In this lazy way they went down the Mere towards Withern and the clear fields that closed that end of the water.

Then, one poling stroke almost brought Christopher out of the boat altogether, and in recovering he sat down and rocked the boat on to a shoal.

'Was that a whale?' said Hugh, who had slipped his mind away from the Mere into the oceans of the world.

'No,' said Christopher. 'It was a deep place. We'll go along it.'

'Just a minute,' said Hugh. 'I'm not ready.' He brought himself back from the southern oceans, where the great whales sail for ever, to the unknown shores of Old England, not far off on the right. 'Ready now,' he said. 'You row, and I'll steer.'

Christopher rowed, and they approached the shore. But the nearer they came the farther off the shore seemed. The deep channel widened out and the water grew dark below. Then there was a boiling rise and heave, and they had passed through a waterhill like the one Hugh had almost trodden in the day before. It threw the boat from side to side, and then they were through it and it was astern: a hump exactly like yesterday's, two feet across, rising to perhaps four inches above water level in the centre, flowing and flowing and not moving away.

'What can it be?' said Christopher.

'I don't know,' said Hugh, trying not to think of the things he had once or twice thought of.

Christopher rowed on. The shore line became clearer. There was a bay here, with a narrow mouth, and the mouth opened sideways to the Mere, so that as they approached it appeared gradually.

'It may be the mouth of a river,' said Hugh. But as they came they saw it was not. Behind a screen of trees there was a grass place, with more trees beyond, and the grass came to the water at the back of the bay.

'This looks like a houseplace,' said Hugh, who had a better chance to view it than Christopher. 'We could live here.'

Christopher rested his oars and looked over his shoulder, and then pulled on again.

'The Bay of . . . ' Hugh began to say, but he was stopped by a splash in the water to his right. When he looked there was only a rising streak of bubbles and a vanishing mark in the water where something had either come up and gone down or only landed and gone down.

Then there was another splash on that side, and a third on the far side of the boat.

'Stones,' said Christopher.

'Bricks,' said Hugh. 'Halves of bricks. And there's the person who's throwing them.'

A fourth stone hit the boat, dented the paint, and fell into the water.

'We'd better go away,' said Hugh. 'That's a giant.'

'It can't be,' said Christopher. A fifth stone hit his left hand oar and skated up it, planing a thin piece off. The blow stung his hand. The sting in his palm and the scar on the oar made him wonder who could throw so far and so hard. He looked, anxious to see where the danger lay so that he could go in the quickest opposite direction.

He saw what Hugh had seen: a huge man with his arm raised to throw a sixth stone. 'It is a giant,' he said. 'He might break our arms with those bricks. Quick, steer away from him.'

Hugh steered, pulling the left-hand cord tight, and Christopher worked with the oars, and they drew away from the little headland where the giant stood.

'Go back into the Mere,' said Hugh. They turned right round and started their slow journey away from the bay. The sixth stone landed ten feet astern. The giant stood in a clear space among the trees and roared at them.

'Were you wishing about giants?' said Christopher.

'No,' said Hugh. 'Honestly I wasn't. I never would. I won't wish again for anything you don't want, Christopher. Or for anything I don't want.'

IX

The Far Shore

CHRISTOPHER lifted an oar over the waterhill when Hugh warned him. Christopher had two things to do now: the rowing, fast rowing, and watching the giant, who stood on the land swinging a half brick gently, watching back at the boat.

'He's stopped roaring,' said Hugh. 'Can I look round?'

'Yes,' said Christopher. 'But don't put out your tongue or anything like that.'

'Then I won't look round,' said Hugh. 'Why do you think of things?'

All the same, after a moment Hugh did look round, and as he did so they ran aground quite hard, and the boat lifted under them and the rudder came off again and floated about.

Christopher got out and let the boat float again and then

pulled it after him as he explored the reef for the deep channel.

'Don't go that way,' said Hugh. 'It gets nearer the land.'

'I've got to find the place,' said Christopher. 'You sit down and shut up. And then when I've found it we'll go back again to where we found the boat and put it away and go to the beach.'

'You can,' said Hugh. 'But I won't. You're allowed to fight giants.'

'And they're allowed to fight you,' said Christopher. But his opinion of the boat and the giant was that they were both better left alone.

'Mind out for those monsters,' said Hugh. 'I expect there's a nest of them under that bubbling place.'

'Crayfish,' said Christopher. But as soon as Hugh mentioned anything it seemed that the thing was not the same as it had been. Not crayfish but some deadly beast; not a borrowed boat but a wished-for one; not trees but people. Yet, the giant . . . they had both seen the giant.

Hugh happily looked out for perils, and was content that his world should be slightly improbable and loaded with what other people would not believe.

Christopher looked in the water closely before each step, ready to climb back into the boat if any creature approached him. He went along the reef towards the shore, and decided that the deep water channel did not lie that way. He turned back, retracing his steps, looking out for monsters, and found the crooked channel in a little while. He fixed the rudder back in its place, climbed into the boat, and rowed slowly out of the bay where the giant still stood, and into the open Mere.

'What shall we find next?' said Hugh. 'Tell me.'

'You're not to wish anything,' said Christopher.

'I won't,' said Hugh. 'I'm thinking of a way to fight the giant.'

'This whole Mere may belong to him,' said Christopher. 'Did you think of that?'

'He didn't say anything about it,' said Hugh. 'But I didn't understand his language.'

Christopher's opinion was that roaring didn't count as language. Hugh said that it did, and that they had been challenged to fight; and that fighting giants was allowed. 'He probably eats people that come his way at night looking for somewhere to sleep: and he boils them up.'

'He could eat us,' said Christopher: when Hugh put ordinary sense on to ordinary nonsense it gave Christopher something to argue about; but nonsense and fancy can't be argued about. The trouble is, the more you argue about the giant's habits the more you believe in the giant.

'He fought first,' said Hugh, 'didn't he?'

'Yes,' said Christopher. 'But . . .'

'It's a rule to fight back,' said Hugh. 'They do at school, don't they? You told me they did.'

'You have to at school,' said Christopher. 'But giants aren't school.'

'But they fight,' said Hugh. 'Now we'll go and land somewhere else and creep up on him.'

They turned towards the end of the lake, where there was the little lawn between the woods where Hugh had imagined a quicksand and got his feet wet. They kept a look-out together for a fence or wall or some boundary that might show the limits of the giant's territory. Two hundred yards up the water they saw a fence that came down and well into the Mere, standing in the shallows like a hollow breakwater.

'That's the end of where he goes,' said Hugh. 'And he's gone away from his battle place.'

'What shall we find this side?' said Christopher.

'Places for houses,' said Hugh. 'When we've defeated the giant and made him into a slave: you can do that sometimes. It would be jolly good to have a slave: better than a lot of African boys.'

Christopher let Hugh's arguments convince him, and began to look for a deep channel to come to the shore again and get on with looking at the giant ready for a fight: he could fight pretty well if he had to, and he won by going on for a long time after the enemy had stopped, so, in time, at school no one bothered him.

The first channel they tried led nowhere, and they had to put the rudder on again and come out backwards. The second opening led them round in a twist and then under the shore to a flat rock that acted as a quay. There was a tree to tie the boat to, and overhanging branches from a weeping willow that hid them from every side.

They stayed in complete quiet for a while: nearly a minute, until Hugh became impatient to move on. They left the boat and stood first on the stone quay and looked into the wood.

The willow had only begun to grow its leaves, and they could see through it into the land. There was a little round lawn just behind it, and then the green leaves of wood-privet and yew, and the brown of ordinary tree trunks. The ground beyond the lawn was covered in ivy, and the trees were draped in it.

Hugh led the way along a path. Christopher thought it might be the giant's walking way, but the branches came so low over it that it could not be so. Once or twice he heard something rustle and move not far away, but there was such a dense thicket of eye-level privet that nothing but the path could be seen.

'Where are we going?' he asked, but Hugh said nothing. He plunged forward until he came to a cross-roads. He looked both ways, and went on, and came to another cross-roads, and then another. At each he went straight over, having looked both ways for ambush. He waited for Christopher after the third, and said: 'Can we find our way back do you think?'

'Easily,' said Christopher. 'We didn't turn left or right, did we.'

'Shall we go back and make certain we know the way?' said Hugh. 'This is so thick that I can't see where the water is at all.'

'We could easily get lost,' said Christopher, agreeing.

This wood was very thick and unknown, and it was as well to learn the paths near the landing place in case they had to go in a hurry. They turned round and went back.

'Straight across,' said Christopher, when Hugh waited at the first cross-roads.

'I know,' said Hugh. 'I'm only looking both ways, in case of the giant.'

'It's too low for him to come in here,' said Christopher. 'Even I hit my head sometimes on the yew branches.'

'He might be snaking about,' said Hugh, and went on across the other path.

Somehow, even in that short distance, they seemed to have missed their way. The next path that went across did not make a cross-roads but a T junction: there was no way straight across; they could only go right or left.

'I thought it was all cross-roads,' said Hugh. 'Shall we go left or right?'

'Right, I think,' said Christopher, and they went right. But round a bend in the path they could go no farther: the path was a blind one with no way through, and they had to turn and take the other arm of the T. This arm led straight on, with nothing crossing it or meeting it, and then tended to the right, and went round in a curve.

Christopher kept an eye on the sun, which could be seen above in the empty branches of the trees. It was first on the left-hand side, and then behind them, then on the right side, and ahead, and on the left again.

'We've come right round,' said Christopher. 'We're facing the way we were.'

'We have to go on,' said Hugh. 'We can't turn off without getting through this hedgy stuff and it's too thick.'

'But we're going in a circle,' said Christopher.

'Never mind,' said Hugh. 'If we go back it'll be the same circle. Come on.'

Again the sun went round, left side, behind, right side, ahead, left side, and they noticed another thing, that the ground was first uphill, then flat, then downhill, then up-hill again.

'We'll go round a third time in a minute,' said Christopher. 'And I can't tell where we are.'

The third time round was flat all the way, but the sun behaved in the same way. They came out of the path into a little clear space with a yew tree in it. Hugh said: 'We've got out,' because he thought they were by the landing-place again. But he was wrong. They were still surrounded by privet hedge, and there were two ways out of the little clearing, two entrances side by side.

'Which one did we come in by?' said Hugh.

Neither of them knew; but with a little careful looking at the ground they decided on the right-hand one as the probable one, and went out again by the left-hand one, unwinding themselves as fast as they could from the mysterious tangle.

Three times round, and they came to a cross-roads.

'Straight on,' said Hugh. 'Absolutely straight on. Remember which it was, Christopher. I want to come out somewhere I know.'

Next was another T junction. They took the right-hand path this time, and at the next junction the left hand, but that began to curve again, and they thought they might lead themselves round and round to the wrong place, so they turned back, meaning to get back to the place where they had turned left and turn right instead: that is, go straight on in this path.

But they came to no T junction (it would have appeared as a path to the right): the path went straight on, and suddenly led them out under the weeping willow where they had started, coming to it by the path they had first taken from it.

'I don't see how we made so many mistakes,' said Christopher. 'Do you think we hurried past places without seeing them?'

'No,' said Hugh. 'I think we kept losing out memories, because that's the sort of wood this is: you don't remember things.'

'Don't be silly,' said Christopher.

'Well,' said Hugh. 'What else could it be?'

'Perhaps the paths are just like that,' said Christopher. 'No, they can't be, because we just turned round several times, and even then the places were different.'

'I've thought of a thing to do,' said Hugh. 'Let's go away before I forget; and I'll pretend I haven't thought of anything until we're out on the Mere again. Anyway, this place is really too low for the giant, so we needn't come back again.'

'But I want to,' said Christopher.

'Hush,' said Hugh. 'Don't let the wood know we want to remember anything.'

X

Lost in Old England

THE blue boat shook itself when they got in again.
Christopher untied the painter from the branch it was
tied to, and pushed off from the stone quay with his hands,
waiting until there was enough room to use the oars.

'I don't like that place,' he said. 'There's something
wrong with it. I *know* we went back the way we came the
first time, and the last time.'

'There were just too many paths,' said Hugh. 'They
muddle our minds, that's all. But I'll tell you what I thought
of, when the wood can't hear.'

'When the wood can't hear,' thought Christopher.
Could it be true that a wood might change its shape whilst
you walked through it? He thought of another thing, and
began to say: 'What if we've been in there for a long . . .'
But he knew that didn't happen: they had not come out
ten years later and thought it ten minutes.

'No,' said Hugh, who had worked out what he meant.
'I don't like that idea: don't let's have it.'

'No, we won't,' said Christopher, and at last had the
boat turned away from the shore and in the deep water.
He found a way of keeping in the channel. If he let the oars
dip deep they would touch the shallow bottom: if they
touched on either side, then the deep channel was in the

middle; but if they touched on one side and sank on the other, then they were too near the shallow side.

In this manner they progressed slowly; though perhaps as fast as they would if they had continually run aground. They did stick once, but gently, and pushed off with oars only and did not lose the rudder.

'Now,' said Hugh. 'If you want to go into a tangly place like that you have to come out again, don't you?'

'Yes,' said Christopher. 'Where are you steering to?'

'Straight across,' said Hugh. 'But if we tied some string to the boat and then went into the wood we could always know where we went by going where the string was, even when we can't remember.'

'We do remember, though,' said Christopher. 'Places can't make you forget.'

'It's better to have a place that forgets than a place that grows suddenly different,' said Hugh. 'Or where it's a hundred years in a minute and things like that. You think of much worse things than me. And more of them.'

'You started it,' said Christopher. 'I only want to think of the things that are real; but I can't think of anything real for that place: it doesn't do real things.'

'They must be real,' said Hugh firmly. 'And we'll get some string and go through them and fight at that giant.'

Christopher's fears of the mysterious wood grew less and less, and the worry that was bigger came back to his mind: whose boat was it? There was another one which he told Hugh: 'What if the giant complains to Mrs Wrigley that we came near him, or even fought him?'

'He won't if we win,' said Hugh. 'You ought to know.'

Then they grounded, and Christopher looked at his watch as it came to his notice on the hand that swayed near his face when the oar waved over the water.

'We'll have to go in for tea now,' he said. 'We've used up all the afternoon in the wood.'

'Only one afternoon,' said Hugh.

'But we mustn't be late,' said Christopher. 'I'm hungry.'

'Go on, then,' said Hugh, 'pull the boat to land. I won't.'

Christopher pulled the boat to land, walking along until he found the deep water and then walking beside it. Hugh kept a look out to the right and saw the waterhill where it had been the first time they met it. He watched it, and then the place where it had been, until Christopher bumped him against the land and he got out. They pulled the *Wish* out of the water, put the rudder and the oars aboard, and their socks and sandals on their feet, and went up through the wood, over the sunk road, down the field called Egypt and back to Mrs Wrigley's. She was waiting for them, softening the margarine and putting aside for Mr Wrigley the strawberries out of the strawberry jam.

'I must say that you boys are very punctual,' she said. 'You've not been late yet.'

Hugh and Christopher said nothing to this praise. Hugh was not impressed by it because he disliked Mrs Wrigley, and Christopher knew that that kind of remark often led into some more that was not praise, and he knew better than to smile. Mrs Wrigley went on: 'There wouldn't be much for you if you were late.'

'I thought there wouldn't,' said Hugh, and went to wash his hands.

'I hope it's not you that teaches him to say things like that,' said Mrs Wrigley. 'You ought to know better.'

Christopher went without saying anything. Hugh was making a muddy mark on a towel with his elbow.

'Was the old witch cross?' said Hugh.

'Only with me,' said Christopher. 'People generally are.'

After tea they were not allowed out of the garden. Mrs Wrigley did not want them in the fields, she said, because it was trespassing.

'I knew it was trespassing,' said Christopher. 'I told you it was all the time.'

'I know it is,' said Hugh. 'But it's not like poaching elephants: they send you to prison for that.'

'So they do you too for trespassing in England,' said Christopher.

'Not us,' said Hugh, and went to find the cat and forget whose it was and play with it. Christopher settled down to some lawful weeding, and Mrs Wrigley, knitting in the window where the sun shone, thought to herself that work would do him good. Christopher, though, did not think it was work; only that it was safe.

Hugh polished the cat so that it loved him well, and when he was sent up to bed it followed him to the edge of the bath; but it went away when he wanted to wash its feet.

Christopher spread a little handful of sand on the

newspaper and drew his initials in it with his finger to spread it. Hugh wrote his on the soap with a nailfile, and they had to wash the soap until the letters were worn away in case Mrs Wrigley saw, so they both smelt strongly of soap when the bath was over.

The blue boat had a spider's web across the bows in the morning. Hugh insisted on going to look at the boat on the way to Withern, where he wanted to buy string. He had already borrowed a long piece from Mrs Wrigley. He had arranged it with the cat, he thought, because a witch's cat is her adviser. But in fact, witch or not, the black cat was the best way to Mrs Wrigley's heart.

'That spider will guide us,' said Hugh. 'Remember not to break its web: it's part of the crew.'

'Part of the boat,' said Christopher.

'The spider, not the web,' said Hugh.

To buy a ball of string in Withern they had to find a shop. By going on through an untried way they found a street of shops and in the street an ironmonger, who sold them a big ball of rough string, all hairy, for a shilling.

The *Wish* was soon launched again, with the spider in the middle of its web shaking at their shadows. Christopher took the oars, and accidentally dropped the painter across the web, so that the spider ran under the bulwarks. He did not tell Hugh, but took the oars again and rowed slowly out into the Mere, touched the shallows on either side until he was clear of them altogether.

'I'm steering for that willow tree that hangs down,' said

Hugh. 'It's an old queen that all the princesses have died of.'

'It doesn't matter where you steer,' said Christopher. 'We shall have to walk along the deep part.'

When they grounded Christopher led the boat to the shore. They tied it up, and got out on to the stone.

'First listen,' said Hugh. They listened, but there was nothing to hear: everything was quiet, and even the wind moved the bare tree-top twigs without breaking into noise over them.

'What shall we tie it to?' said Christopher. 'If things move we ought to tie it to something that doesn't.'

'The *Wish*,' said Hugh. 'What have you done to the spider? That was silly. Anyway, the boat won't move away, and if it does we can still come back to it. I'll use Mrs Wrigley's string first, because it's thicker than what we bought.'

He tied the string round the thwart, and led the way into the wood. Christopher followed him, but first he broke off a willow twig and cut the bark at one end on one side with his thumb nail, so that at each crossing or junction he could note down, with his thumb nail again, which way they had taken.

'This is exactly the way we went yesterday,' said Christopher. 'I remember these cross-roads.'

They had crossed all three by now, and Mrs Wrigley's string came to an end. Hugh tied it to the fluffy bought string and let that trail. They looked back at it, lying on the path and showing certainly which way they had been.

'Let's go back, the same as we did yesterday,' said Hugh. 'I want to see if we have forgotten.'

The string led them straight back to the boat: there was no mistaking its good value. 'I knew I was right,' said Hugh. 'They ought to use string more often.'

They went on again, beyond the three cross-roads, Hugh letting the string down again from the loose bundle he had gathered it into. They passed over the known ground, turned a corner, and came to a junction, but either arm of the junction was blind, and they had to go back to the third cross-roads. Christopher's willow twig was useless now, because for one thing he had forgotten what the marks meant, and because half of them were no good. He threw the stick down.

They took the left-hand turning at the first cross-roads and laid the string gently round in the middle of the path.

'If we'd measured it we could tell how far we'd been,' said Christopher. 'We ought to have tied a knot at every yard.'

They turned right at another cross-roads, and then right again, and in a moment came on their string again.

'Now we know where we are,' said Hugh. 'We can't get lost.' They turned and went back to the last cross-roads, and went on, as if they had turned left when they first came to it.

Wherever they went they laid the string, until they came to the end of it. Hugh put the end down and stood on it. 'We must go back now,' he said. 'We can start again, and you can draw a plan of where we go.'

'I haven't a pencil,' said Christopher. 'Or a piece of paper.'

Just as he spoke there was a noise in the wood: a creaking squeaking scraping bumping noise, then a quiet pause, and the same noise again, and a door banged. There was a little more quiet, and something sneezed.

Hugh and Christopher looked at each other, wondering what or who it might be.

'Him,' said Hugh with his mouth and not his voice. 'Giant.'

There was a noise of quick footsteps, running not far off. They stopped. Hugh and Christopher peered into the hedges on either side, and over the hedges, waiting for a huge figure to look over at them.

'Let's go back,' said Hugh, and bent to pick up the string.

It was not there.

XI

Discussion

Hugh lifted up his heel, and sticking to it were a few white threads from the rough string, ringed with moist earth colour where he had trodden them down: they looked like hair from a tortoiseshell cat.

'I haven't forgotten the string, I did bring it,' said Hugh. 'But we're lost again.'

'But it wasn't the wood,' said Christopher. 'It was some-body who took it away.'

'The giant,' said Hugh. 'And we've nothing to fight with, not even a sword.'

'We could go and spring on him,' said Christopher. 'It's

twice he's attacked us.' He thought now that the giant was playing fair, and after challenging them twice was obviously ready to fight in an ordinary way and not turn on them and order them about like a headmaster, or a headmaster's mother.

'Will you fight now?' said Hugh.

'Yes,' said Christopher. 'He's insulting us, not bossing us, so we ought to fight.'

'I've said so all along,' said Hugh. Christopher privately thought that Hugh had a lot to learn about what to do when you are attacked by different kinds of people for different reasons.

This conversation was very whispered with heads close together, and when it was done they listened all round, and heard nothing; looked round and saw nothing: there was still the same morning silence. They walked back the way they had come, until they were at the first crossroads. They shook their heads and shrugged their shoulders at each other: they had no idea how to go now.

'Do you know,' said Christopher. 'These hedges have been cut: that's why they're so thick.'

'That would make them thinner,' said Hugh.

'Like a garden hedge,' said Christopher. 'It keeps them thick because they grow inwards instead of outwards.'

'Does it cut itself?' said Hugh. 'If it grows where it wants it could cut where it wanted.'

'I mean, it's all done by somebody,' said Christopher. 'The giant, I suppose.'

'Then come and find him,' said Hugh.

Wherever they went they were lost. The paths led everywhere and nowhere. Once they tried to keep a check on their direction by watching a yew tree's high top; but though they went round it they never came to it, and at last they lost it.

'We're caught,' said Hugh, and sat down under the hedge to think of it.

'No,' he said, in a little while, 'we aren't so very lost. Look under the hedge, Christopher.'

Christopher came down to Hugh's height, and looked where he looked. Beyond the ivy-grappled roots of the privet he saw another path, running alongside the one they were on. And on the other side of their path was a third path.

'Not thick bushes,' said Hugh. 'We could get through to that path,' and he began to tug at the two-inch-thick trunks of the hedge. But there was no bend in them, and they scratched at his hands as he tugged.

'They'll be loose somewhere,' he said, and moved along the path, trying to push his way through. Christopher lent his weight and his hands, and they went along attacking the unforgiving hedge.

Then one trunk slipped away from another, the top of the hedge swung, and a section fell over, leaned against the next hedge, and left a gap.

'It's held in with wire,' said Christopher. 'And one end is in the ground. It's not a real hedge.'

'But it is on either side,' said Hugh. 'Come on, let's break some more down.'

They pushed through the gap they had made, and then stood the section of hedge up again. When Hugh kicked the bottom of it he found metal under the ivy, and a tin box that held the privet's roots.

'I think,' said Christopher, 'that somebody ran about near us and put pieces like that in when we had gone past, to muddle us up and make us think it was a forgetting wood.'

'The giant, of course, teasing us,' said Hugh. 'I think he will fight very badly; perhaps he's afraid of humans.'

They were out of the wood sooner than they expected, because, prospecting along the path, they suddenly came across the end of the string. Hugh caught it before it moved away, but even when he had it it did not tug. He and Christopher held it, and they followed it, rolling it up again into a ball like wool.

It led them out to the willow tree, and there was Mrs Wrigley's string tied to the boat as it was before. They were so pleased to see the boat that they went to it and sat in it before the wood lost them their way again.

'That's that,' said Hugh. 'We'll have to walk along in the water until we get to the giant's place. But I wish we had a way of getting through the wood because that's the proper way to him, I know: it always is the proper way to go through a place like that.'

'Don't wish about it,' said Christopher. 'You know what happens when you wish things.'

Hugh said nothing to this; but there was an answer. It came from a third voice, which said gruffly: 'Why not wish?'

Christopher immediately put both hands against the stone where the boat lay and pushed hard. Hugh did not think of going away. He picked up an oar and held it in both hands and stood up, but went down again into the bottom of the boat when Christopher shook it. The oar fell into the water. The boat shook again when the painter pulled it up, and they were no farther away than they were when Christopher pushed, and wetter, where the oar had splashed.

The owner of the voice slid down a weeping willow branch and landed on the stone beside the water.

'Oh, a goblin,' said Hugh, from his upside down place in the boat. 'No wonder about the wishes.'

'A goblin, yes,' said the person on the stone. He was very short and wrinkled, but he was thick and strong and heavy too, and stood squarely on the stone looking down at them. 'You can never tell who lives in woods and might be listening to your talk.'

'We didn't know it was your wood,' said Christopher.

'You aren't the giant who's changed his shape, are you?' said Hugh. 'Don't tell a lie.'

'I am always this shape,' said the goblin. 'And I know about the giant: I think it ought to be a good fight. I've always wanted some helpers, because I've never won yet.'

'Is he your enemy too?' said Hugh. 'We'll help you as much as we can, won't we, Christopher?'

'Yes, of course,' said Christopher, still not believing that the little person was a goblin. But there was nothing else he could be.

'Come ashore,' said the goblin. 'One's Hugh, and the other's Christopher, I think.'

'Me, and him,' said Hugh. 'Now tell us about the fighting. Have you any magic things?'

'Come with me and we'll have a discussion,' said the goblin. 'Discussions and cups of tea are what I most enjoy, next to a fight with the giant, of course.'

He pulled the boat in and steadied it whilst Hugh and

Christopher landed. Then he stood up. He only came to Hugh's shoulder.

'You found out my trick,' he said. 'This isn't the giant's wood, but mine, and I have it like that to keep people out: particularly the giant, who would be quite a nuisance otherwise. Of course, I know the maze very well, and when anyone comes in I go after them and close up the gaps until I've led them where I want them. Sometimes they become very wild and frightened.'

'We did,' said Christopher.

'Nothing wrong in that,' said the goblin. 'What I don't like is people who are frightened too easily. Now, you never looked frightened.'

'We keep being frightened,' said Hugh.

'A very good thing to be,' said the goblin. 'But as I say not so good to look it. Now you follow me, and we'll go to my place and make a plan for the overthrow of the giant.'

He led the way into the wood, turning left and right, so often that neither of the boys had any idea of the way they had come when they reached a door that was not in a hedge but in a cliff. The goblin looked first at his watch, which was an ordinary wrist watch, and then took a key from his trouser pocket. They were ordinary trousers such as any man would wear, but small. He had a brown pullover with long sleeves, and brown hair that stuck up on top of his head in a steep wave. He unlocked the door, and pulled it open. It made the groaning, creaking, squealing noise that they had heard earlier in the wood.

Beyond the door there was a dark tunnel, with light coming from the far end. The goblin closed the door they had come through, and they were in almost darkness. He led them on, and they found it lighter and lighter until they came to a door on the right, where they went in. It was the door to a little kitchen with a burning stove to one side and a row of little windows to the other. The ceiling was low for Christopher, but safe for Hugh. Christopher bumped his head on a beam, and the goblin offered him a chair to sit in. It was a small chair, but he sat in it, and looked out of the window.

There was a wood outside, and there were squirrels leaping in the trees, and in the clear spaces below the trees half a dozen great black birds walking, and under the window two budgerigars standing on a stick, and at the other end of the wood was a stumpy square animal, brown and black, digging slowly and looking for something. It was a bear.

The goblin filled a kettle, not from a tap but from a deep bowl of water in the corner of the kitchen, and when he had filled it the bowl was as full again as it had been. Hugh was on his knees in a corner playing with a nest of white kittens.

The goblin shook the fire in the stove and put the kettle on top, brought three cups from a cupboard, a jug of milk, sugar, and a teapot.

'What are they doing out there?' he said. 'Is that bear still digging?'

'Yes,' said Christopher. 'And the black birds are helping.'

The goblin opened a little piece of the long window and
called from it 'Sugar'. The bear stopped digging at once
and came running on all fours to the window. The
budgerigars flew away, and the black birds went on looking where the bear had dug.

'I don't give him much sugar,' said the goblin. 'Only
very little, but he likes it.' There was some very hard sugar
in a box. Christopher had thought it was gravel or quartz,
but the bear took a lump from the goblin's hand and
crunched it and swallowed it. The goblin shut the window,

and the bear tapped for more.

'Go and dig,' said the goblin, and the bear went to dig.
'My little family,' said the goblin. 'I wish elephants were
smaller, and then I would have one: they're very pleasant
in their natures.'

'Haven't you any dragons?' said Hugh.

'Not this year,' said the goblin. 'They seem to be scarce
at present. Now, is that kettle boiling?'

XII

Royal under the Skin

THE goblin made the tea and put it on the table.
'I hope you do not mind eating biscuits from a
shop,' he said. 'We goblins find shops so useful that we
forget how to make biscuits and bread, and all the things
we ought to know how to do.'

'Are there lots of you?' said Hugh. 'Or is your family
only animals?'

'I'm the only one in this district,' said the goblin. 'We
were never very common anywhere. Do you take
sugar?'

So they sat drinking tea with a goblin on an April morning, whilst the goblin asked them who they were and
where they came from and how old they were.

'How old are you?' said Hugh. 'I always wanted to
know how old a goblin was.'

'I'm about forty-five, in goblin years,' said the goblin.
'But they aren't the same as human years. But now I know
all about you and that you're staying with a witch, and we
must get on to serious business: the giant.'

'What is his name?' said Christopher, because he wanted
to be able to note him down accurately in his memory.
The goblin thought before answering.

'He hasn't a name, so far as I know,' he said. 'If there
were several giants I think they would have names, among

themselves, anyway, but where there's only one, then he's the giant. The Giant of Withern Mere, I suppose, to pick him out from the rest of the world.'

'Not even called Grumbleblow, or Mancrusher?' said Hugh.

'No, nothing like it,' said the goblin. 'Now, how did you first meet him?'

'He threw stones at our boat,' said Christopher. 'One of them hit it, and another hit the oar, and we only just got away through the waterhill.'

'I know the thing you mean,' said the goblin. 'But what had you done to the giant to cause him to throw stones round you? He could have sunk the boat if he had wanted: he's a dead shot with a stone or a catapult or an arrow. Had you annoyed him a little?'

'Not at all,' said Hugh. 'He threw halves of bricks, anyway, and roared loudly.'

'I see,' said the goblin. 'Perhaps he thought it was me. You see, it's my boat, and he might have thought I was disguised, or had changed my shape.'

'Can you change your shape?' said Hugh. 'Change into something now.'

'I was never very good at it,' said the goblin. 'I stopped that sort of thing several years ago. I'm not a very successful goblin, you see: if I had been I would have dealt with the giant long ago; and been able to change into anything I wanted, as well. I'm only an animal-keeping, gardening, cave-digging kind of goblin, and I only travel about in the summer: most goblins travel in the winter when the weather's at its worst and few men are out because the horses don't like it.'

'You can always go in trains now,' said Christopher. 'Or by car.'

'New inventions,' said the goblin. 'Not the sort of thing for my race at all. But we mustn't keep wandering from the subject. You were in my boat, you say?'

Christopher felt that some correction was about to be made: whose boat was whose, and things like that. Every borrowing without careful permission was like that.

'Oh, yes,' said Hugh. 'Thank you for granting my wish.'

'I did what I could,' said the goblin. 'I didn't in fact know you had wished for a boat; but I knew it would be useful to your Highnesses.'

Hugh sat up straight at that, being a prince as fast as he could, wondering which crown to wear that day. Christopher thought it best to be honest about it, though he would like to have been a prince too. 'But we aren't Highnesses,' he said.

'It's sad in some ways,' said the goblin. 'In the old days they were all princes; but now they aren't, though they're just the same to look at. I quite thought you were of royal blood and hadn't liked to mention it in case of some trickery or other. Never mind, so long as the boat was what you wanted.'

'Just right,' said Hugh. 'We wanted to find a place where our father . . .'

'The king,' suggested the goblin.

'The king,' said Hugh, 'might build a house—a palace, I

98

mean; and we thought this side looked better than that side, and we *do* want to live at home in a house, and we hate Mrs Wrigley.'

'And the giant knew nothing about that, I suppose,' said the goblin. 'No, he wouldn't, of course. I agree with you that this side of the Mere is the best, and only the giant and I live here. His house is quite a big one.'

'It would have to be,' said Christopher. 'Tall people have tall houses.'

'And small ones small houses,' said the goblin. 'You could never crack your head on his roof tree; but I didn't dig this cave any deeper than I had to.'

'Is it really a cave?' said Hugh. 'Perhaps Dad—the king, you know—could dig a cave as well.'

'There's plenty of room for a house,' said the goblin. 'The giant's house used to have a great garden all along the Mere; but since he's come down in the world and isn't so rich, the garden isn't used, and a house could easily be built anywhere down there—except in the maze, of course, where you were lost.'

'Can we go and look?' said Hugh. 'I've finished my tea.'

'The giant is still roaming about,' said the goblin, shaking his head. 'And we don't want to be caught by him until we've worked out a way of dealing with him. Besides that, there's one thing that will have to be done before anyone thinks of building a house here. You'll have to find water, your Highnesses.'

'Water?' said Christopher. 'What about the Mere? That's pretty full of water.'

'It's not drinking water,' said the goblin. 'It's not house-water at all. And now and then the sea gets into it and poisons everything.'

'Do waves come on it then?' said Hugh. 'And storms?'

'A little,' said the goblin. 'But I was telling you about the water: you'd have to find somewhere about a spring that you could use. I have a little spring here, and that's why my cave is here.'

'We could use that,' said Hugh. 'It could go into a pipe instead of into that bowl.'

The goblin shook his head. 'I'm afraid it's only a very small spring,' he said, 'but it's very good soft water and the sea never gets into it. Most of the water here is hard water, and the sea might get in at any time. You can't be certain it won't until you find a high-up spring above the sea.'

Christopher thought that the course of events would be to vanquish the giant, then find water, and then find a place for a house; and after that see whether Dad would build one there. The goblin thought they should find water first.

'We can only beat the giant,' he said. 'We can't finish him off for ever. We shall have to make an arrangement with him, you see, about what land your royal father wants: giants are very particular about their territories, and so are kings; and we must be careful not to take more than we want for the palace. We must know where it is, and then we can fight.'

'It seems like war, just to fight for a thing you want,' said Christopher, remembering a day of war at school that had ended sadly with the stick all round, not for fighting so much as for greed: and all for a little piece of garden that grew an apple tree that was destroyed in the fight. The goblin knew about giants though, and said it was the rule to decide what you wanted to buy from them. 'But it's no good if you don't win,' he said.

Hugh wanted to know how to find water, and where it might be, and could they do it before dinner? The goblin looked at his wrist watch, and said there was no time before human dinner time, and that he would tell them afterwards what to do, if they came to the landing-place under the weeping willow. 'It was an ordinary willow once,' he said; 'but it saddened over something and has wept ever since.'

Hugh put back a lapful of white kittens with their mother in the corner by the stove. The goblin opened the door, and they followed him out, Christopher stooping to avoid the beams in the roof of the cave.

The bear was still digging gently, and the black birds were round it talking gently in grating voices, and the squirrels still leapt high in the trees.

They walked into the darkness of the passage, to the door. As soon as it was opened and closed noisily again the goblin sneezed. 'I always do,' he said. 'I think the light gets into my nose: light's not what it was in the old days.'

He led them through the maze to the boat, untied the painter, and pushed them off. 'I'll be waiting for you with a plan,' he said. 'I wish you a happy journey, your Highnesses.'

When they were clear of the reef Hugh said: 'I'm glad I'm a prince. I didn't think of it before.'

'You aren't a prince, though,' said Christopher.

'If everything else is true that happened, then I am,' said Hugh. 'It can't some of it not be true if it all is.'

'Well, it's not the same as school,' said Christopher. 'That's all; and I'm used to school.'

'I'm used to this land,' said Hugh. 'It's good and dangerous. Saying we didn't win the giant fight? We should have to go on and on all the rest of our lives, and that would be something to do. We should be in the books, like Jack.'

The boat grounded on the farther edge of the deep water. Christopher pulled it round to the channel and rowed it in. They drew it on to the shore and hurried up through the wood and through the hole that grew larger and larger and more and more comfortable the oftener they went through it.

There was a moment of danger in the road, when they had to stalk Mrs Wrigley home, and not appear near her too suddenly, in case she realized that they had come through the hedge. They followed her in, and Hugh insisted on sitting at the edge of the lawn and emptying imaginary sand into a flowerbed. Mrs Wrigley told him to do such things no more, because the salt was bad for the roses. Hugh apologized and went to wash his hands. Christopher spent ten minutes brushing from his clothes the white fur from the goblin's white cat. Mrs Wrigley would have been highly suspicious of it if she had seen it.

The black cat was suspicious in any case, only by smelling Hugh; but that did not matter, because Hugh gave it a gravy-covered plate to lick so that it would say nothing to Mrs Wrigley: it was likely to, he thought, if it was a good witch's cat.

Free from Mrs Wrigley at last they left the garden, climbed the field called Egypt, ran down to the boat, and left behind the usual world. Hugh took to it easily, because it was the sort of world he invented. Christopher took to it slowly, because each time he came he had to re-examine the facts about it: they seemed unnatural facts, and unnatural facts too often seemed to have been imaginary facts with trouble beyond them. Hugh's ideas about things being what you think they are gradually came to his mind, and the excitingness of them seemed less and less to mean danger of later punishment from ordinary people.

'Swords, I think,' said Hugh. 'Shall I row?'

XIII

Six Springs

T HE goblin met them under the weeping willow.
'Good afternoon,' he said. 'Don't tie up and get out,
because you'll be on the water this afternoon.'

'Attacking?' said Hugh. 'You can sit beside me.'

'We can't attack yet,' said the goblin. 'I explained that
to your Highnesses. No, this afternoon you must look for
water. Until we've found water we cannot decide how to
attack the giant. So you must go out into the Mere and
find the seven springs that keep it full; and when you've
found them we will see what sort of water flows from
them. But it's only once in seven years that they can be
found.'

Hugh was dismayed at that thought: 'Can't we have a
small fight first?' he said. 'Why wait seven years?'

'Do what you're told,' said Christopher, repeating
school's most important rule.

'They are reckoned to flow one day in every seven years,' said the goblin. 'But I find they come more often than that. At present they have been flowing strongly for more than a week, but they are getting less strong now. The rule is to find them all in one day; and I think it can be managed in an afternoon. Now, you discover where they all are, and we'll find out what kind of water comes from each one before it's too late. They may not be there tomorrow.'

'Not at all there?' said Hugh.

'Not there so that you could see them,' said the goblin.

'But how do you see them?' said Christopher. 'Where are they?'

'Let me see,' said the goblin. 'They're under the water, but there's no water on top of them. That'll do to guide you, I think.'

'I know,' said Hugh. 'Are they all like that?'

'They are today,' said the goblin. 'Come back when you've found them, and I'll be here.'

He gave the boat a push, and watched them navigating the narrow channel, and then turned and went back into his mazy wood.

'I wonder what dangers there are,' said Hugh. 'I ought to have borrowed a sword. We know two waterhills already so we only have to find five.'

'Waterhills?' said Christopher. 'Of course: they're made of water, and there isn't any more on top of them. We know two of them, and they're both near the edge of the Mere, and perhaps the others are too.'

'We needn't visit the giant's one again,' said Hugh. 'We don't want him to know we might be thinking of attacking back. We'll pretend to be friends if he sees us.'

'That wouldn't be fair,' said Christopher. 'We'll pretend to be frightened of him and go away.'

'It would be safer,' said Hugh, 'to . . .' But he did not say what he thought was safer.

When they had rowed up to the head of the Mere, where the first lawn was that they had ever found, they turned and looked down the water. 'We've got to find five little things in all that,' said Christopher. 'All in one day. Do you think we can?'

'We don't row quick enough,' said Hugh. 'I think we ought to walk along the shallow bits and row along the deep bits; but only if I can row and you can walk.'

'If you want,' said Christopher. 'But you must come to me when I call you and not be too far away, and don't get stuck on the other side of the lake where I can't come to you, or fall out, or get wet.'

'Don't fuss of me,' said Hugh. 'You go and walk about: they only come once in seven years.'

The afternoon passed slowly, with nothing to mark the passing minutes and hours as they fell away. Christopher, first on the south side of the water, found nothing between the head of the lake and the channel that led to the weeping willow. After Hugh had rowed him across the deep part he went on, and found three waterhills, one of which was the giant's one: he saw it in the farther deep water, then went back again a safe distance and had Hugh ferry him right across the lake, and from there he worked up to the head of the water again and found two more waterhills, which made five altogether, because it included the two known ones.

Hugh drifted about the Mere in a haphazard way, mostly engaged in seeing mermaids or cities or wrecks in the water. Then, when he was thinking that water could be as thin as air and if some was the boat would sink, the boat lurched and spun, and there was the sixth waterhill under his oar in the middle deep of the Mere, which was a part he was sure he had examined.

He consulted with Christopher, and they counted up their scores, checking where each hill was, making certain it was six.

'One more to get,' said Christopher. He got into the boat and put his feet in the warm sunlight. 'Those six weren't difficult, because they were all close together. But the last one might be anywhere at all, mightn't it?'

'Right down near the town, perhaps,' said Hugh. 'We couldn't look at it all in a day.'

'We've only got three-quarters of an hour before tea,' said Christopher. 'But we'd better go down there and see what we can find.'

So they went down the lake, leaving the wooded shores and coming where it was marsh at the edge and mud below, and thick and reedy everywhere, and in one place there was a flooded wood with sluggish water between the rotting stumps and quiet splashes of hidden animals hiding as the *Wish* came near.

'I don't like this place,' said Hugh. 'I think there are things in it.'

'We ought to go back anyway,' said Christopher; but his real reason was not time: Hugh made his fancies sound real and threatening.

They rowed up the centre of the Mere, round the far side of Beaver Island, where they had not been before, pulled the boat over the reef, came to the weeping willow and found the goblin waiting for them.

'How many?' he said.

'Six,' said Hugh. 'We went down to look for the seventh, but we only found a forest that was in ruins in the water with things in it.'

'I shouldn't go there,' said the goblin. 'All the springs are up here somewhere. If you'll come ashore, your Highnesses, there will be some tea in my cave.'

'We can't come,' said Christopher. 'We never asked Mrs Wrigley.'

'The witch wouldn't let us come,' said Hugh. 'We have to go back there for her to fatten us up with her food before she eats us.'

'A very difficult situation,' said the goblin. 'But what else can you do? We don't want her made suspicious and asking the giant for help. I'm afraid I've always been her enemy: she doesn't like me at all; though her husband often would talk to me. But I don't like to go where I'm not welcome. But do your royal parents, the king and the queen, know that you are being fattened by a witch?'

'The witch is our mother's friend,' said Hugh.

'I have a friend who is sometimes a scorpion,' said the goblin. 'And another who is very probably a witch, and there is nothing to be done about either of them: they're my friends, and I have to help them when they ask me. That's a disadvantage of being a goblin: you never know whose side you'll be on next.'

'But you're on ours now,' said Christopher. He thought this was like a rebellion against school and the masters, but the goblin thought it was different: he would not join them in any fight against Mrs Wrigley.

'I'm on your side,' he said. 'But I can't be against your mother's friends, even if they're dragons by night. If I wasn't a goblin, perhaps I might: I don't know.'

'But she's your enemy already,' said Hugh.

'That makes no difference,' said the goblin. 'I'm not on either side when it comes to you two. It's my duty to be a goblin now, and the better goblin I am the better I'll be when I change.'

'Change?' said Hugh. 'I thought you said you couldn't.'

'I can't do that kind of change any more,' said the goblin. 'But goblins are only the caterpillars of some other kind of thing; but of course we don't know what. I want it to be a good thing. I don't suppose it will be, because I'm not a very good goblin, though I keep the rules. I'm lazy about doing the clever things such as changing and doing my own baking and digging up metal. I haven't even a large enough cave, and if a lot of visitors came I should have nowhere to put them. But you don't want to know what kind of goblin I am.'

'Oh, we do,' said Hugh. 'We like you.'

'Thank you,' said the goblin. 'But all the same, I can't help you with Mrs Wrigley: she isn't a friend and she isn't an enemy, and that's all there is to it. Come back after tea and we'll see about the seventh spring: we're bound to do it tonight.'

They made a quick journey by boat to the other side of the Mere, ran through the trees, and came in a few minutes early, and kept out of the way until tea was quite ready. Hugh started badly by taking the wrong dish of jam and eating five strawberries set aside for Mr Wrigley before being found out. He said he was sorry so well that Mrs Wrigley forgave him and scolded Christopher instead for dropping his knife.

After tea they went out without permission, running through the fields called Tunisia and Libya and through the hole in the hedge of Egypt, and crossed by boat to the weeping willow.

The goblin was waiting for them with a basket. 'Make room for me,' he said. 'The giant has gone to plunder some villages to the south, and he won't see me with you. You go on rowing, Christopher: you're getting to know how it should be done. Hugh is not good at it at all, I fear.'

'Let me do it now,' said Hugh. 'I don't always want to do it properly; but I could if I wanted.'

'Not today, your Highness,' said the goblin. 'We must have our best rowers on the job today. Pull out to the middle of the Mere, Christopher, and we'll think where the spring might be.'

'Don't we just look?' said Christopher. Hugh at the same time wanted to know what was in the basket the goblin had brought.

'One at a time, children,' said the goblin. 'In the first place, we must look where you haven't already looked; but where you have been in fact. And in the second place, I have brought some jars to bring away some water from each spring and see what they are like. But we must find the seventh. Whilst we think of where you have been and yet not looked we will visit each of the others and take water from each.'

Hugh took over the rudder then, and Christopher told him how to go, and they crept from waterhill to waterhill, waiting at the edge of the shallows whilst Christopher took a jar—they were honey jars with screw tops— to each spring and held it in the surging deep and let it fill with the newly rising water. He did not leave the boat to dip at the spring in the giant's bay, where they had been when he bombarded them, but leaned over the side of the *Wish* and filled the jar from there. There were three jars to fill from this side of the Mere, and when they were done, and put in order in the basket and a number scraped on each metal top, they began to cross the Mere.

'Oh,' said Hugh, when they were half-way across. 'Beaver Island: it's the only place we've been to once and not been to today.'

'But we didn't see a spring,' said Christopher.

'Nor hear one?' said the goblin. 'Are you sure?'

XIV

Seven Springs

WHEN they heard again the sound that they had called Beavers there was no mistaking it for anything but water, underground water. Hugh wanted to move the top of the little hill and make the seventh visible to the world; but the goblin said no, and made them study instead for a way in without digging.

'Get the water where it comes out into the lake,' said Christopher at once. The goblin agreed, but Hugh thought that was too tame to be proper, and wanted to make some mark in the place.

'Christopher's way is right,' said the goblin. 'Why show everybody the way to the spring? I dare say it's hidden for a good reason.'

'I dare say we don't know what the reason is,' said Hugh. He began to pull turf from the hill, and very soon came down to stone, and then a gap in the stone, and when he had dug the earth out of the gap his hand came out wet, and from the newly made hole came the boiling noise of fast water and the spray of a bottled spring-head.

'A fountain leaping to get out,' he said. 'Can't we open it?'

'Certainly not,' said the goblin. 'This island belongs to the giant: we mustn't let him know there's anything valuable on it, for one thing, because if he wanted a fountain he could have found it himself.'

'Fountained it himself,' said Hugh.

'Yes,' said the goblin. 'If you like. And we mustn't do any damage in case he wars against us before we're ready.'

'We can take the water from this hole, though,' said Hugh. 'Give me the jar.'

He put his arm in through the gap for trial, then pulled it out and put the jar through, brought that out full of water, screwed the top on and gave it to the goblin.

'Fill up the hole again,' said the goblin. 'It would be better covered.'

Hugh listened once more to the cold boiling of water, looked in to see whether there was light there, and sealed the hole again.

'That's the strongest spring,' said Christopher. 'Do you suppose it's the highest one that doesn't get sea water in it?'

'I think that may very well be so,' said the goblin. 'A sister spring to the one in my cave. But we must take water from the three other springs, if you will be so good as to show me where you found them.'

'Easily,' said Hugh. 'I'll steer and Christopher can walk about.'

When they had visited all the surface fountains, and arranged the bottles in the basket, the goblin suggested a visit to the giant's castle, on his side of the water.

'We'll have to be quick,' said Christopher. 'Mrs Wrigley didn't say we could go out now.'

'An awkward state for two young princes to be in,' said the goblin. 'But it has its advantages: the giant will be sure that you are enchanted in some way, and possibly even slaves of the witch.'

'Is he a friend of hers?' said Hugh.

'Not really,' said the goblin. 'But I don't think they've ever quarrelled. By the way, you haven't been enchanted, have you?'

'Not me,' said Hugh. 'Christopher has, a bit, I think, but he's better than he was.'

'What at?' said Christopher.

'Not being the witch's slave,' said Hugh. 'You always do what she says: even her gardening.'

'She grows flowers,' said Christopher. 'Why not?'

'I should think that she has another plot of ground somewhere where she grows only weeds,' said the goblin. 'Witches have that habit, you know.'

Then he told them to be quiet whilst he rowed them across the Mere and into the darkening bay where they had first seen the giant.

The still trees stood round the still water, and the gold sunset clouds were plaited in their branches. The little blue boat looked whiter and whiter in the dusk. It reflected itself more and more strongly in the water as the light went out of the sky.

The goblin grounded them against a little beach, so that they stepped off on to the grass without getting their feet wet. The goblin dragged the boat up from the water, because there was no branch near to tie the painter to.

'No talking,' he said. 'Follow close behind me, and don't be afraid of anything.'

They were between the water and the trees now. When they reached the trees there was more grass beyond, and beyond that grass again dark woodland. They crept from tree to tree and felt that they were being watched and were on a skyline. Ahead was a wood with a grey depth to it, and trees that brushed the sky. They left the fringe of trees and they were in the grey wood following a path.

There was a leafy thicket in front now, and on either side the enormous roots of the sky-touching trees. The goblin crawled now, and then wriggled along flat under the thicket. The boys followed, and the bush held their hair and caught their elbows and it all felt like a trap that would close and cut them up with its ten thousand thorny knives.

Their faces came out of the dragging twigs, and there was clear ground ahead: they were even clear of the wood. More grassland lay in front, and there was a courtyard full of giants and giant beasts.

'Take no notice of them,' said the goblin in a twilight whisper. 'He only does it to frighten us. Come on.'

He crawled out of the bush and stepped forward ten feet to the foot of a giant looking at the sky. But the giant did not move, and when Christopher and Hugh followed him and joined him there they found the giant was cut in a bush of yew and was in every way as silent and still as if it were solid wood.

There was a forest of giant shapes, and they dodged from one to another, with the goblin looking carefully all ways before moving. Then they came to the end of the grassy courtyard of monsters and there was a wall covered with creeper, and the goblin began climbing the creeper without warning.

They followed up the thick laddering stems where there were no leaves yet, and stood comfortable at the top looking over the wall.

Beyond was the castle. It was a square building with a tower at each corner, and it was battlemented all round.

'He's let the moat dry up,' said the goblin. 'Lazy, I think. That's the front door.'

They all three had night eyes now, and they could see the narrow windows all round, the black door, the dropped drawbridge, and the hollow ditch of the moat.

'No light, no smoke,' said the goblin. 'Still out, I dare say.'

'No,' said Hugh. 'Look, listen.'

At the corner of the house there was a change in the shadows, and the giant came walking round his castle, and after him ran some small animals, darting here and there in his footsteps. The giant came to his door, pushed it open, and went into the blackness. The door banged behind him and the little shapes gathered at the door, still scattering and gathering, but not going away.

'Peacocks,' said the goblin. 'I hope they don't hear us. Go down quietly, because he'll be out again soon to lock them up. I've tried many times to catch one of those birds, but they've always warned him.'

They were nearly on the ground again when Christopher thought he was, and let go with his hands. He landed on the grass with a springing thump, and the loose creeper he grabbed at snapped loudly and stayed in his hands.

'Quickly,' said the goblin. But they heard the peacocks scream in the garden beyond, and the door open.

'Run,' said the goblin, and they ran among the yew figures and through the wood to the boat, pushed it out and fell into it.

The goblin took the oars and pulled for the mouth of the bay, staying close to the shore all the way.

There was a thundering of footsteps in the wood, but they were round the little headland where the giant had thrown his stones, and aground on the reef, out of sight from the bay.

'Be ready to abandon ship,' said the goblin. 'Though it's too dark for him.'

But there was no need for more alarm. The footsteps came out of the wood, stood still, and then went back, and after a while they heard the castle door bang again.

'Safe,' said Hugh.

'Yes,' said the goblin. 'But now you know. Sometimes he hides among his statues: all he needs to do is stand there, and he catches you as you walk past.'

The goblin pushed off from the land again, and rowed them across the Mere to their landing-place, without ever touching the shallow bottom. 'Run home,' he said. 'I'll take the boat and meet you in the morning.'

'We're awfully late,' said Christopher. 'There may be an awful row.'

'You'll have to brave it,' said the goblin. 'If I were you

I should go into the fields the other side of the road and not let her think you've been here.'

'It's all right,' said Hugh. 'I'll cry, and she'll blame Christopher and not me.'

'I hate being blamed, even if I did do it,' said Christopher. 'Can't we tell her the truth?'

'I think it would be quite impossible,' said the goblin. 'I mean, she wouldn't listen to you, would she?'

'No,' said Christopher. 'But lies aren't right.'

'It's all right,' said Hugh. 'She doesn't want to know, because she doesn't like us except to eat when we're fat. I'll cry, like I said, and we'll be all right.'

'Good night then,' said the goblin. 'Good luck.'

Mrs Wrigley was certainly very angry, and did not

want to be given explanations. She waited until they were getting into the bath before slapping them, and went downstairs feeling that they were well punished.

'I've got a tough bottom,' said Hugh. 'I don't mind.'

'I don't mind that,' said Christopher. 'I just don't like people cross with me.'

Mrs Wrigley came up again later on and lectured them on causing anxiety, but they were in bed then and in the dark and had no need to listen. When Mrs Wrigley had gone down Mr Wrigley came up—he was sent by Mrs Wrigley in his slippers and still holding the newspaper.

'Derum where you were trub mine abow,' he said, and left them.

'Please,' said Hugh.

'Dwansing?' said Mr Wrigley.

'Give my love to the cat,' said Hugh.

'Soo?' said Mr Wrigley. 'Nigh.'

He closed the door and went downstairs again.

'I don't understand what he says,' said Christopher.

'Slave language,' said Hugh. 'Bewitched, you see, and enchanted.'

'Oh, shut up,' said Christopher, and felt the place where the ground had been when he fell off the wall, and the other side where Mrs Wrigley had slapped. Hugh was only half bruised in comparison. His anger at Hugh's imaginings vanished as he went to sleep.

XV

Word with the Enemy

'You can't go on the sands on a Sunday morning,' said Mrs Wrigley. 'Surely you know that.'

'It seems to be ordinary weather,' said Hugh. 'Is it a Sunday too?'

The argument came at breakfast-time because neither Hugh nor Christopher had put on the clothes Mrs Wrigley brought them when she woke them: they had dressed in yesterday's.

'At school we get up later on Sundays,' said Christopher; but Mrs Wrigley thought that remark insulted her household.

'I hope you wear your best clothes,' she said. 'And it

would be a funny school that didn't take you to church.'

'We go to church,' said Christopher. 'It costs three-pence, and the headmaster puts in a shilling, and the organ squeaks when it isn't being played and we all laugh when nobody's looking.'

'You ought to know better than that,' said Mrs Wrigley. 'You should behave properly in church.'

'I've never been to a church,' said Hugh. 'In Africa there aren't any and we go to other people's houses on Sunday and we often go on the beach.'

'After breakfast you can go up and change,' said Mrs Wrigley. 'And then you can come down and sit in here and keep clean until it's time to go.'

'We said we'd go somewhere else,' said Hugh, remembering that the goblin was meeting them with the *Wish*.

'You're not going to play on the sands on a Sunday morning,' said Mrs Wrigley. 'Now go and change and sit still until Mr Wrigley's got the car out.'

Hugh was much puzzled by church, because no one had ever told him anything about it. Christopher was not puzzled, though he knew nothing about it either, but he had become used to it, Sunday by Sunday at school. Mrs Wrigley met all her friends, and they talked in the church-yard afterwards. Christopher and Hugh stood beside her to be shown to people.

'The singing sounded like Africans,' said Hugh, when they asked him how he was enjoying his stay in Withern; and they did not ask him again what he thought of anything.

'You behaved quite well,' said Mrs Wrigley, 'but there was no need to mention natives, Hugh.'

'I know about Africans,' said Hugh. 'They don't, do they?'

As they were getting into the car by the churchyard gate there was a heavy footstep behind them. Mrs Wrigley was in the car then, at the front, and Hugh was waiting until the back door was unlocked before getting in. At the sound of the heavy footstep both boys looked round, and there was what they had thought of: the giant; and he dropped a great hand on each right shoulder.

'Good morning,' he said. 'I hear we are to have a fight soon.'

'Yes,' said Hugh, clenching his fists at once. 'Against you, Mr Giant.'

'I shall look forward to it,' said the giant. 'I've heard all about you, and I hope you enjoy yourselves whilst you are here.'

'We are,' said Hugh. 'Except for some things.'

'Good-bye,' said the giant, and he let go of their shoulders and went up the street with great strides.

'Well,' said Christopher.

'Get in,' said Mrs Wrigley. 'What are you waiting for?'

'Talking to somebody,' said Hugh. 'We know some people already.'

Christopher sat in the back of the car and heard no more of anyone's conversation. He was sorting out all the muddling facts that had appeared to him, starting with the goblin and ending with the friendliness of the giant. It was easy, he thought, for Hugh to think they were slightly magic; but whatever Hugh thought or imagined there was no magic, no sudden land of goblins and giants and princes beyond the Mere. Yet they had been there, without any sort of fancying at all, and seen the goblin and the giant, and been called princes. If you added it up and looked at it it seemed true that they were in another country beyond the Mere. Yet again, if the land was there, why had the giant spoken to them in such a friendly way? How could it all be so?

The explanation came to him gradually: it had to, because it troubled his mind all the time to find himself in a place he did not believe in. If the goblin pretended to be a goblin, and the giant pretended to be a giant, and really they were friends . . . But they are goblin-sized and giant-sized . . . Yet they are only pretending, and playing a game, and we are playing it too . . . Hugh always played things as a game . . . The game had either come to life, or goblin and giant were playing it with Hugh. And with me, he thought. If I play it instead of trying to make it into sense, will that be better?

It was better, he found at once. He looked at Mrs Wrigley in the front of the car, and found she was a witch, quite certainly . . . Pretending certainly, that is. And Dad was a king . . . That could very likely be so, because he was a kingish man used to ordering people and sending them to do things.

Hugh pushed him out of the car at the end of the

journey. 'We've got time to go and look, haven't we?' he said.

'Not before dinner,' said Mrs Wrigley. 'Now you sit in the garden and remember it's Sunday.'

'I know that anyway,' said Hugh, 'Can we put our best clothes on?'

'Those are your best clothes,' said Mrs Wrigley.

'Our best for wearing,' said Hugh. 'These are Sunday ones and we might easily get them dirty in the garden.'

Mrs Wrigley made them sit in deck chairs, and would not let Christopher nurse the cat, because of its loose black hair.

After dinner they were allowed to change and Mrs Wrigley let them go, glad that they needed so little amusing. They made sure she was not watching, and that Mr Wrigley was out of sight in his greenhouse, then crossed the field called Libya into the one called Egypt, climbed through the hedge and came down to where the boat usually was.

'He's come and left it,' said Hugh. 'Good. I hope he didn't have to wait long: he might have left a spell on it so that we turn into something.'

'You get in first then,' said Christopher. He had practised his mind into thinking that the goblin might be as real as you pretended him, but no more; and the answer pleased Hugh.

'We ought to try it with a dog,' he said. 'That's what they usually try things on.'

'Wish for a dog,' said Christopher. 'Or shall I?'

'No,' said Hugh. 'This will do,' and he found an earwig, which chased over his hand and then fell into the boat, and ran under the thwart.

'Seems all right,' said Hugh, and looked under to see how it was getting on. 'Still there,' he said. 'And still the same shape: that's all right too.'

They launched the boat, and rowed in their natural shapes across the Mere.

'We had to go to a meeting of witches this morning,' said Hugh. 'That's why we're late.'

'Witches always meet in churchyards,' said Christopher.

'And we had to go to see what it was like,' said Hugh. 'People don't often go and come back alive, but we did.'

'They only took us to eat,' said Christopher. 'Luckily they weren't hungry.'

The goblin was asleep on the stone quay when they towed up to it. He woke up when Hugh called 'Good afternoon' to him.

'Good afternoon, your Highnesses,' he said politely.

'We went to a witches' meeting this morning,' said Hugh. 'We couldn't get here at all.'

'So did I,' said the goblin. 'A goblins' meeting, in fact; but I left a note in the boat, and took it out later when you hadn't come.'

'Written on a piece of bark?' asked Christopher.

'Certainly,' said the goblin. 'With vultures' blood: that's the proper ink.'

They tied the boat and came ashore. The goblin offered to show them the secrets of the maze, so that they could use it as a refuge if they met the giant or another enemy anywhere.

'I took the jars of water to an alchemist I know,' he said.

'When he's finished his present experiment, which is finding out how to make gold, he'll see which is the best water. I think it is very important to know a good reliable alchemist. It'll be a bad day when they succeed in making as much gold as they want, though.'

'Why?' said Hugh. 'Won't they share it with us?'

'Never,' said the goblin. 'But they wouldn't do anything for us at all, like making bat-wing plaster and grinding hair for putting on wounds or forecasting weather—and telling us what's in the water from the seven springs.'

The afternoon was used up in exploring the maze thoroughly and learning it. After an explanation of its general plan the goblin took them through it to his door and made them lead him back to the willow tree, and to the door again. Then, having learnt this main road, they learnt the road to the borders of the giant's garden; and the way into the inward twisting track that led only to its own small central lawn. They learnt how to move the sections of hedge from place to place so that the roads were changed. By tea-time they knew how to get themselves out of any place in the maze, and learnt how to recognize each path. It was simple in construction, in fact, with four quarters, and the spiral to one side; and the quarters were all exactly alike.

'I cut it every autumn,' said the goblin. 'It takes me a month. It used to be done by three gardeners from the giant's house, and it was built to amuse people, not to be a hiding place for enemies. But that's what happens to ideas: they get turned against you.'

Hugh wanted to know when they could use it for the fight, and when the fight would be. Most of all he wanted to know what they should fight with.

'An army,' said the goblin. 'I'll get one. We wouldn't have any chance without one, because he could take forty or fifty of us in each arm and crush us. We'll use the army to confuse him on all sides, and then we'll close in and deal with him.'

'What sort of army?' said Hugh.

'I have my friends,' said the goblin. 'Creatures I know.'

'Crabfish,' said Hugh. 'I know. But don't let them come near me.'

'We saw the giant this morning,' said Christopher. 'He said he was looking forward to the fight.'

'Yes,' said Hugh. 'We were just getting on to our broom stick, so we couldn't wait. He was tearing the tops of the houses off and eating people inside for his dinner.'

'Very likely,' said the goblin. 'A bad habit of his. If we go down to the Mere now we may see him fishing for his tea: he often does on Sundays.'

'I'm glad we aren't out there,' said Hugh.

'You could always pull the arrow out,' said the goblin. 'What's a wound or two to a prince?'

They went to the shore—Christopher showed them the way through the maze to the willow. Then they kept among the trees until they crossed the fence whose end was in the water, and could see the mouth of the bay where the giant lived. 'Wait,' said the goblin.

In a few minutes' time the giant came to the shore with a great bow on his shoulder. He watched the water for a while, then raised the bow, slid an arrow on to it with his thumb, pulled the string back to his shoulder, and fired into the Mere.

'How will he get it?' said Christopher. But the answer was obvious at once: there had been a string on the arrow, and the giant pulled the string up, gently, dragging in to land what he had shot.

'He generally loses it about now,' said the goblin; and as he spoke the giant roared gently but angrily, and pulled the string in quickly with the arrow dropping water.

'He could walk into the water and get it,' said Christopher. 'Even if it was deep he's deeper.'

'I think it makes him weak,' said the goblin. 'He'd be no good for hours if he got wet. He'll get tired of fishing if he doesn't catch anything soon. But you can't go until then, or he'll sink you. He's a perfect dead shot with a stone or a boulder.'

'Or an arrow,' said Hugh. 'Look, he's got another.'

'And lost it again,' said the goblin ten seconds later. The giant dragged in his empty arrow once more, rolled up his string, and went away.

'Not very patient today,' said the goblin. 'Bad temper, I dare say. Well, you'd better be off now, and I'll see you in the morning, and we'll have a plan of campaign, and probably have the fight in the afternoon and take possession of the giant's lands until he gets too strong again. Good-bye for now. Be careful how you go, your Highnesses.'

XVI

Plan of Battle

'I WISH Sunday evening would end,' said Hugh, long after tea, when they were kept in the garden. 'I think she's gone to sleep and forgotten about us.'

'It's too dark to weed any more,' said Christopher. 'Shall I go and wake her up?' But they dared not, and when the wind blew cold they went in quietly and put themselves to bed and Mrs Wrigley had merely to come and put out the light and say they were good boys.

'Giant fight tomorrow,' said Hugh. 'I'm thinking about it.'

Christopher thought about it too, and the thought went to sleep with them, and woke them thoroughly when Mrs Wrigley called them in the misty morning with the sunlight visible in it.

After breakfast they left without asking, because Mrs Wrigley had a look of inventing occupations for them. They were out so early that they had to wait for the postman at the gate and let him past: he had never brought them anything yet, so his load did not interest them.

The boat was waiting for them, with a new web spun by the same spider as before.

'It's spun itself a maze,' said Hugh. 'We can use it as a plan to go through by.' But they had no need of a plan, because between them they knew their way through the wood, and they came to the sticking door that led to the goblin's cave without being lost for a moment.

The goblin came out of his kitchen when he heard the door being pulled, and came to welcome them. He closed the door behind them and said 'Good morning, your Highnesses. Very good battle weather don't you think?'

'Yes, very good, very good indeed,' said Hugh, being the colonel-in-chief for a moment.

'Good weather makes a fight so much more comfortable,' said the goblin. 'Come into the kitchen. I've not quite finished with the family yet. Then we'll look at the places where the fight will be, and see which piece of ground you want from the giant, and the alchemist will be here at eleven, and we'll come in again to hear his report.'

The kitchen was full of great black birds, standing on the floor and on the table. They would not move for Hugh and Christopher, and had to be pushed aside. They all moved when they saw the goblin, and crowded round him nodding.

'My ravens,' said the goblin. 'They have to live in a cage most of the summer, and plenty of people look at them, so they aren't shy and they don't mind being indoors. What they want now is something to eat. I'll feed them outside. Watch from the window and see how obedient they are.'

He said to the birds 'Follow me', and the birds said one after another 'Yes, Mr Gray', and walked out of the room after the goblin.

There was a door leading to the woodland before the

window, and the goblin led them through that. The squirrels came very close to watch what happened. A little way down the wood the bear sat in a chair at a table, eating very politely and wearing a bib round his neck. The bear finished eating, got down from the chair, pushed it under the table with his shoulder, and sat down on the grass to watch the feeding of the ravens.

They stood in a row, and the goblin stood in front of them with a basin in his hand. 'First bird,' said the goblin,

and the first raven walked to him in its stiff-booted way.

'My name is Dolly and I want my breakfast,' it said.

'Good girl,' said the goblin, and threw down a handful of lumpy food.

'Thank you, Mr Gray,' said the bird called Dolly.

Each raven came forward, said its name and that it wanted its breakfast, and thanked the goblin, in the name of Mr Gray, for it.

Then the grave birds were fed, and the goblin came in to

give the white cat some milk and meat and count the white kittens. 'In case the ravens have been naughty.'

'I think the bear will tear its bib,' said Christopher.

'Oh, will you take it off for me?' said the goblin. 'His name is Bunny.'

Christopher went out to meet his first bear, who came to meet him, and took hold of him, but he only wanted to look heavily in Christopher's pockets, and whilst he bent his head Christopher undid the strings of the bib, and brought it back. The bear hiccoughed and sat down again on the grass.

The goblin had finished his work and swept the room when he came in, and Hugh was stroking the kittens smooth and letting them crawl on his fingers. 'I wish water felt like this,' he said. 'Soft and silken and warm.'

'Come on,' said the goblin. 'We'll look at the battle-field, and we'll look at the place I think you'll like, where there's room for a house.'

'And a garden,' said Christopher.

'Both,' said the goblin. 'Complete with neighbours— me and the giant.'

He led them along the edge of the Mere, the way they had gone when they watched the giant fishing. But they went beyond their watching place, and came out at the place where the giant had thrown his stones from. Beyond was the bay, fringed with trees, and beyond the trees the lawn they had seen twice but never examined.

'That's the place,' said the goblin. 'Both for fighting and for living in. We'll crawl along the edge of the wood and look at it. But first the battle. Now, the object is, as I expect you've guessed, to put the giant in the water where he'll be no more good. So I'll put the army near the water here, leaving a wide space in the middle clear, and we'll drive him down from the wood, there, where he'll come out, to the water. He won't be able to escape along the edge, because of the army, and we only have to come to him and plunge him in.'

'Only,' said Christopher. 'Is it easy?'

'No,' said the goblin. 'But we can try, can't we? It'll be hard, but I reckon we'll do it.'

'If your army's any good we'll be all right,' said Christopher. 'We can rush him over into the water.'

'The important thing is to get him to the water,' said the goblin. 'We can do that; and the rest's fighting in any case, wherever we are: it can't be helped.'

When they had in this way reviewed the battle in whispers they went up the edge of the wood, looking at the wild lawn in its trees.

'Gently sloping, dry, facing the island,' said the goblin. 'The spring water will come up to the top of the house easily: my spring is much higher than this. There's a road out there beyond the trees. It's sheltered here, sunny, and quiet. I don't think there could be a better place for a palace.'

'And we could keep this grass instead of a garden,' said Hugh. 'And we'd have a boat, not a car.'

'We'd better go back now,' said the goblin. 'The alchemist will be waiting for us, and it doesn't do to keep them waiting if you can help it: they get impatient and start leaving magic about. I had a lot of trouble once with a chair that kept changing into a cactus, after I'd made an alchemist wait half an hour.'

They hurried back to the cave, and the alchemist was waiting there. He was an ordinary sized person and he had to move about on bended knees all the time.

'I walked in,' he said. 'I hope you don't mind. I used the All-Purpose Key, a new invention of mine, quite invaluable to every person in the habit of visiting, priced at only two months.'

'Really?' said the goblin. 'May I introduce the alchemist, your Highnesses: Prince Christopher and Prince Hugh.'

'Very pleased and very proud to act in any way for their Highnesses,' said the alchemist, bowing as much as he could without falling over, because his knees were bent so already.

'Which was the best water from those seven springs?' said Hugh, wasting no time on talk.

'The jar labelled Four, your Highness,' said the alchemist. 'I found it a delightfully soft, pure, clear, moist, cold and in other words fresh liquid, and quite the best I have come across for some time.'

'Four,' said the goblin. 'That would be the island jar, your Highnesses.'

'Yes, it was,' said Christopher. 'I scratched the jars and I remember.'

'Apart from a little honey in one other I found nothing

nice in them at all,' said the alchemist. 'There was sea water in three and grit in three.'

The goblin filled his kettle and put in on the stove. 'Would your Highnesses allow the alchemist to sit?' he said. 'I think he bumps his head often, and,' he whispered 'it doesn't do to spoil the alchemist's temper.'

'Of course,' said Hugh. 'Sit down, alchemist.'

'Thank you, Highness,' said the alchemist. 'Now, I wonder if I could interest you in a Neverfail Everfull purse, in pigskin with gold mountings, price two years three months?'

'What does it do?' said Hugh. 'And I don't understand the price.'

'It always has money in it,' said the alchemist. 'And the price need not worry your Highnesses: one of your subjects could do it for you.'

'I still don't know what the price is in money,' said Christopher.

'Payments to an alchemist are generally made in service,' said the goblin, from the cupboard where he kept the cups. 'The purchaser helps in the workshop for the length of time he mentions. But naturally your Highnesses would pay some other person to do the work.'

'I see,' said Hugh. 'But I wouldn't mind being an alchemist's helper. What else have you got?'

'If two people came would it be half the price?' said Christopher. 'Have you got anything that only costs a morning?'

'Ah,' said the alchemist, 'do your Highnesses wish to

purchase something? Of course, I could let you have some things for nothing, if you would allow me to display your royal coat of arms and put "By Appointment to their Highnesses" on my notice board.'

'We'll see about that,' said Hugh. 'Tell me what you've got first.' And they listened to the alchemist's stock of useful magic items whilst Hugh imagined himself a coat of arms.

XVII

Starting the Fight

'ENJOY yourselves,' said Mrs Wrigley. 'Don't be late for tea.'

'No,' said Hugh, and hurried after Christopher. Christopher was walking fast because he did not want to think.

'What will it be like, the battle?' he said. 'What will it be like?'

'I don't know,' said Hugh. 'It's got into my dinner and I don't want to fight.'

'Run, and shake it down,' said Christopher, who felt the same about it but was more used to violent events in the future getting into the dinner he had just had.

They made good time through Egypt, down the wood, and across the lake. The goblin was waiting for them at his door in the maze, and the alchemist was still with him.

'I felt it my duty to stay, your Highnesses,' he said. 'There are so many little services I could offer; and I did not feel it my place to go when I had not been dismissed.'

'Are you on our side?' said Hugh.

'He certainly is,' said the goblin. 'But I don't think he's a valiant man, by any means.'

'No fighter,' said the alchemist. 'But I am able to provide many useful things for use in battle. Nonsqueak Rustless Armour, for one thing, seven months an outfit; or Knocko Boxing Gloves, at thirty days, guaranteed to knock out.'

'Some of them would be useful,' said Christopher. 'What would it be best to have?'

'The Moustache of Invisibility you told us about this morning,' said Hugh. 'Then we could do some stalking.'

'But that was two years two months,' said Christopher.

'And you don't get it until afterwards,' said the goblin. 'Besides, the alchemist has nothing with him, and the battle ought to start very soon. We'd better go and call the giant out.'

The only thing he brought with him this time was a white cloth. They walked through the maze, losing the alchemist twice on the way, when he went looking at the ground or the leaves. The third time Christopher caught him, and then kept him in front. They came out in the wood, and when they had passed through the wood they were on the chosen battleground. Christopher, still pushing the alchemist in front of him as they walked across, mentally laid out a rose bed and a place for a rockery.

'One of you two, your Highnesses, will have to go to the castle and tell him that the time has come to fight and defend his honour,' said the goblin.

'*I* couldn't go,' said the alchemist. 'It would be altogether too valiant.'

'It isn't your job,' said the goblin. 'I know how to arrange fights. I think Prince Hugh ought to go. You must take the flag with you and tell him to come out and take his chance against us. He can't do anything to you whilst you hold the flag; and of course you can't do anything to him, though you can say what you like.'

'I will,' said Hugh. 'Then I'll come back.'

'Good,' said the goblin. 'Now I think we'll steal a little of the giant's property,' and as they went through the wood beyond the clearing he cut a stick and tied the white cloth to it.

'Go in front now, Hugh,' he said. 'Take the flag. We'll come with you as far as the wall, and then you must go alone.'

'Yes,' said Hugh. 'Do I knock at the door?'

'If you have to,' said the goblin. 'Don't go in, though: white flags are only outdoor things.'

Hugh pressed his stomach, where his dinner lay sad within him, took the flag from the goblin, and led the way out of the wood.

They came among the monster shapes of the yew trees, keeping an eye on each, in case the giant was there pretending to be one of them. But he was not. The nearer they came to the wall the slower Hugh walked, until the goblin held the others back and said to Hugh 'Go on'.

Hugh straightened his back, held the flag high, walked through the tall archway in the wall, and out of their sight. They stood quietly and waited.

Hugh saw the square castle in front, and the tall doorway beyond the bridge. There was no one about. He went on, and nothing moved anywhere. Perhaps the giant was out. But he saw that the great door was a little open, and knew that someone must be at home.

There was a sudden scream; but it was a peacock, and when he had trembled once he went on in the same line, towards the door.

Hugh was content to believe anything he fancied, and even if the belief and the fancy led him into what looked like danger he could not turn his back on what he had done: he was truly frightened now, and yet the danger of going on was less than the danger of turning back, because, after all, this might not be a game any longer. Perhaps it never had been a game.

The door of the castle opened, and out stepped the giant. Yesterday morning's friendliness had gone. He looked terribly, and he stood terribly and he walked terribly, and he came to Hugh, bent over him and said terribly: 'Where do you come from?'

Hugh said 'Um', first, and then he said 'I came by myself to challenge you to a fight, and it's no good breathing over me and stamping because you can't touch me.'

'Why should I touch *you*?' said the giant. 'I don't think

I could fight you.
Where is the enemy?
Bring him to me and
let me see him.'

'I *shall* be fighting
you,' said Hugh. 'And
my brother, and a
goblin we know, and
an alchemist we met.'

'What a gang of
fearful ruffians,' said
the giant, and laughed.
'I cannot trouble my-
self with a small fight
today, little messen-
ger.'

'You've been chal-
lenged,' said Hugh.
'Are you frightened?'

'Not I,' said the

giant. 'But I'm not interested. Off you go, before I pickle
you and put you with the others.'

'Are you giving in without a fight?' said Hugh. 'You
coward.'

'Shrimp,' said the giant, and walked into his castle
again. 'You're not dangerous enough.'

Hugh waited for him to come back, but the door closed
firmly, and there was silence again. Hugh turned round
and came back to the garden of tall yews.

'He refuses to come and fight,' he said. 'He doesn't think we're dangerous enough.'

'He's conceited,' said the goblin. 'It's often the case with an elderly giant. I thought it might be so. It's up to Christopher now.'

'Give me the flag,' said Christopher.

'Not the flag,' said the goblin. 'Take this,' and he handed Hugh a small bag. 'There's grain in that. You go and bring all the peacocks here, whilst I go and get a sack to put them in. If he doesn't notice anything we'll give him a shout when I come back; and if he notices before that and comes after you, take a peacock each and run into the woods in different places, and wait until I bring the army.'

The goblin turned and ran for the wood himself. 'Throw away the flag,' he shouted over his shoulder. 'This is war.'

The alchemist and the two boys were left. They looked through the archway at the castle. It was quiet, and all was still.

'Go on,' said Hugh. 'The peacocks are near the far corner.'

'I'm going,' said Christopher, and started across the giant's inner garden.

He walked two hundred paces to the corner. The peacocks shrilled at him at the seventy-fifth step, at the hundred and eighth and at the hundred and forty-second. After that they began to come near, inquisitively.

There were three of them with great fanning feathers, and a fourth that was a dull bird. They stalked proudly to him, and when he scattered a little grain on the ground they ran at it greedily and came to him for more, and began to follow him back.

Every ten or fifteen paces he threw down a little more, and as the birds came more and more quickly they lowered their argonaut plumes and scampered after him.

Then he was safely with the others, and leading the birds through the giant figures, and he had not been seen.

They went into the wood before they dare speak.

'Well done,' said the alchemist. 'The spoils of war, I think. I have always wanted peacock feathers: they come in very handy ten times a day for this and that.'

'We haven't won yet,' said Christopher. 'The goblin knows what to do next.'

'Er, you two go and find him,' said the alchemist. 'If you will permit me to make the suggestion. And I'll look after the peacocks.'

'No, it's all right,' said Hugh. 'Here he comes. Who's he got with him?'

There was a small square figure walking beside the goblin, and behind them walked six more short black ones.

'The bear, and the birds,' said Christopher. 'Are they his army?'

They were the army; and whilst the goblin lined them up and kept the ravens from the peacocks he told the humans what to do.

'I'm going to put these down by the water,' he said. 'They'll stop any escape into the wood. Whilst I'm doing that you must take the peacocks and go back to the arch over there and give a great shout, and show yourselves stealing his birds. Hugh, you must shout loudest and say what you like, and when he comes you must let him follow you. Run out into the battlefield, and lead him down to the water. And from then on we must just fight for all we're worth, and hope that we've got him in the right place before we begin.'

'I see,' said Hugh. 'But you'll have a rescue if he catches me early, won't you?'

'Certainly,' said the goblin. 'Now, do your best.'

He went away with his band of animal soldiers, and the peacocks were led again to the door of the castle garden.

'Shall I shout first, your Highnesses?' said the alchemist. 'Now, if I had brought my Voice Strengthener, a bottle a day—I mean, a day a bottle—we could have broken the windows from here.'

'I'll shout,' said Hugh, and he took a breath. Then he let it out again and picked up a peacock first and tucked it under his arm. He took another breath, and shouted 'Daddy Long Legs without any peacocks. Come out and fight.'

'Come out and fight' seemed to be a good battle cry, and they all three shouted it together, two or three times.

The castle door opened. The giant came out.

'Have you lost anything?' shouted Christopher; and 'Coward, coward,' shouted Hugh. They turned the peacocks round so that their long feathers might be seen. The alchemist shouted in his poor voice 'Peacocks for sale, peacocks for sale.'

The giant stared at them for a moment. Then he

stretched his great hands and suddenly started to run towards them.

There was a scramble in the gateway, and the alchemist got away first, holding two peacocks. Then Hugh and Christopher were among the clipped trees, and the giant was in the gateway. The alchemist had gone into the wood, and one peacock and the dull bird, the peahen, were left.

'Where are they?' said the giant, looking for Hugh and Christopher, not the birds. 'I see you,' and he ran towards them among the yews.

Hugh said 'Leave him to me,' and waited until the giant had passed him, then shouted 'Who's lost his hens?' and began a dodging game among the trees, with Christopher watching and standing by in case of need.

XVIII

Fighting the Fight

Hugh hugged for a second the solitary leg of an armoured soldier, swung himself round it, and sheltered behind a griffin. Christopher watched from six trees away. The giant followed Hugh, trying both to catch him and to get between him and the wood, so that he could be driven back to the castle.

Hugh did not see the danger, and thought he could lead the giant where he wanted, if he could make enough speed. He retreated along the grass between the trees, but soon came out from running straight and into the dodging again: the giant was much faster on the straight, but in the trees he could not follow Hugh's tight turns.

The goblin was in the wood, watching now. He called to Christopher, and Christopher went with him, and left the panting chase.

'Will he be all right?' said Christopher.

'Oh yes,' said the goblin. 'They'll be through in a minute. Come and get into your battle place.'

The battle place seemed to be anywhere in the battlefield. Among the trees near the water stood the bear, fastened with a chain to a tree. He was at the right-hand end of the thin band of trees, and at the left-hand end the trees were thick with ravens: all six were there, watching the setting out of the battle.

Christopher chose a place near the wood that Hugh would come through. He had an idea of ambush, but the goblin would not discuss it. 'No time,' he said. 'They'll be here at any moment,' and he went himself to stand in the middle of the clearing, with the alchemist beyond him again looking the other way and contemplating escape into the safe woodland beyond.

The desperate chase among the clipped trees went on in silence. Christopher anxiously looked through the wood; but there was nothing to be seen but the trees and a little idea of light beyond.

Then Hugh came panting through like a hunted hart, and, looking behind and seeing that no one was there behind him, he flung himself into a bush and lay there gathering his breath.

Christopher went into the wood to him. Hugh took up a breath and said with it: 'He goes like a lorry,' and could not speak again.

'Where is he?' said Christopher. Hugh pointed back the way he had come and went on with his strong breathing. There was no one to be seen in the wood, and nothing to be heard. But there was a little bell-like noise far off up the clearing, and a shout from the goblin.

'Enemy in sight,' said the goblin at the top of his growling voice, and Christopher ran out of the wood.

'Come soon,' said Hugh, and began to manage to breathe without moving his arms.

The giant was coming down the battlefield at ten miles an hour on a huge bicycle. He carried a lance and a shield, and did not use his handlebars, and he was bearing down on the goblin, who stood on a little hill and watched.

Christopher ran to him. 'When he comes,' said the goblin, 'you run to the left, and I'll run to the right, and he'll fall off because of the bumpy ground. Then we'll start.'

The giant came on, growing larger and larger in Christopher's eyes, until he filled the sky and the lance was very close.

'Go on,' said the goblin, and ran to the right. Christopher sprinted to the left, well clear, and turned to see what was happening.

The bicycle was running on empty, and the giant stood on his feet, gripping the lance and shaking the shield, which was in fact a small cupboard door with the knob still on. The bicycle went on like a runaway camel, until it tipped on to its own spinning pedal and collapsed and lay still with a whirring back wheel in the air.

'Dead horse,' shouted the alchemist, who was coming at a run to the rescue of the goblin who was walking backwards from the point of the lance that circled a yard from his face.

'At him your Highnesses,' shouted the alchemist, and flung himself on the lance, at the side, of course, not on the point. The giant juggled with him for a moment, and then sent him hurtling in seven somersaults over the field. The alchemist got up and ran towards the water. The goblin was ahead, and when the alchemist caught up they rallied and turned to face the enemy again.

The giant was now watching Christopher with the point of the lance, and bringing him round with airy jabs, from which he naturally edged away, until his foot kicked metal, and there was the bicycle, trying to trap him. The lance struck air again, and Christopher jumped over the bicycle, picked it up by the saddle, and used it as a shield. The giant fenced at him with the lance, until he seemed satisfied with the position he was in, then lunged, but Christopher thrust the bicycle forward, and the lance went through the wheel. Christopher heard it scrape beside him, and his arm touched it, but he pushed the bicycle on and on, because the lance's point was safely beside him. He suddenly found himself against the giant, with the bicycle saddle rattling against the shield.

The giant dropped the lance and put a sudden great hand over the bicycle; but he was too late: Christopher was already moving away. The bicycle and the lance fell at the giant's feet, and his hand caught nothing.

'Well done,' said the goblin, close beside Christopher, and laid hold of the lance. Christopher helped, and the alchemist put his hands on it, and pulled the lance through the bicycle, and they had captured it.

'Throw it in the Mere,' said the goblin. 'Where's Hugh?'

'In the wood,' said Christopher. 'Getting his breath.'

'He ought to be by the water,' said the goblin. 'Tell him, but put the lance in first.'

Christopher ran off, with the heavy lance trailing, whilst the goblin and the alchemist danced round the giant teasing

him and keeping him where he was by jumping on the
bicycle, a thing that seemed to annoy him, because he hit
the goblin a great ringing blow that sent him starfishing
round in a circle. The alchemist, very indignant, pounded
on the shield with raised and clenched fist until the giant
pushed him flat on to his back.

The giant used the seconds that they were on their backs
to climb on to the bicycle again, and begin to ride down
the field.

Hugh came out to Christopher. 'What's the matter?'

said Christopher, because Hugh's face was red and his eyes wet.

'I was laughing at the fighting,' said Hugh. 'It was the funniest fight I'd ever seen.'

'It was a jolly serious one,' said Christopher. 'I've got to put this lance in the water.'

'Why?' said Hugh. 'Let's both take it and charge at his legs.'

'The goblin said put it in the water,' said Christopher.

'We'll just do it once,' said Hugh. 'Oh, he's on his

bicycle again. We could knock him off easily, so let's try.'

Two people on a lance might be effective, Christopher thought, so they turned about, and held it at the ready against the advancing giant. The giant bellowed at them.

'Angry,' said Hugh. 'We'll knock him out and throw him in the water and hold him down until he's got no strength left.'

The goblin and the alchemist picked themselves up and came behind the giant.

'We'll get him down they can jump on him hold tight,' said Hugh in a breath. He was behind and pushing, and they ran towards the giant.

The giant left the bicycle again and ran on waving his shield. Then he stood firm, whilst the lance came on at knee level. Christopher realized that it would never hit him; but the giant bent down and put the shield in the way, and knelt to take the shock.

All three went over at the blow, and they trampled the giant, lost the lance when it stung itself out of their hands, and found themselves flattened on the flat shield.

The giant was sitting up, and they flung themselves at his neck. The alchemist and the goblin joined in before the giant had raised himself farther than having the palms of his hands flat on the ground: almost sitting. All four of his enemies attempted to push him down again; but they were not prepared for his sudden collapse, and when they went down with him he wrapped his arms round all four and stood up, holding and crushing them whilst they wriggled and kicked.

'What we want,' said the alchemist, whilst the others grunted and writhed, 'is an eight-day Expanding Unbustable Vest, guaranteed to withstand all pressure . . .' But he had no such thing and the giant squeezed out all his breath.

'Bite,' said Hugh, and bit the giant's thick arm. The giant snarled and dropped all four.

'One at a time now,' he said. 'Peacock thief first,' and he stretched out his arm for Hugh, and dropped the shield.

'You know where to go,' said the goblin. 'Come on, you others.'

Hugh knew where to go. He ran for the trees and the water, with the giant after him, shaking off Christopher who was at his knees. The alchemist lugged at the lance, and brought it with him, following last of the army.

Hugh came down to the trees, and did a little more dodging amongst them, but the giant would not come through until the alchemist butted his ribs with the thick end of the lance. The giant snatched the lance and hurled it through the trees and into the water, and the alchemist sat down looking startled. 'You next,' said the giant. The alchemist still sat.

Hugh went to the water's edge. 'Peacocks,' he said. 'Who's lost his . . .' The taunt brought the giant through the trees and close to the water.

'Where we want him,' said the goblin. 'Now or never,' and went in to attack.

The giant realized his poor tactics, and ran to the right; but there was the alchemist running with him the other side of the trees; and then the giant came to the bear, who looked at him, remembered his duty, stood up and bared his teeth, snarled, and brought his claws up ready to hold whoever came.

The giant turned away, leapt over Hugh, and ran for the other end of the grass strip. The alchemist and the goblin paced him on the other side of the trees. The ravens were at the end of the grass strip, and when the goblin called to them they left their branches, glided through the air, and attacked the giant with their beaks, so that he put his hands up to protect his face. The ravens bit his fingers, said among themselves 'Down with giants' and beat him back to the middle of the strip. He had his hands over his face now, and did not see where he walked.

'All ours now,' said the goblin. 'Trip him up and push him in. Enough, my children.' The last words were to the ravens, who left the giant and settled on the grass. The giant saw Hugh and Christopher just in front of him, and stretched out to take them, but as he did so Hugh scrambled under his feet, and Christopher jumped at him. The giant tottered, fell gradually off balance, caught at Christopher as if that would pull him up, found he was no good, and snatched Hugh instead: there was nothing else to hold; neither of them was any use to him, and with a mounting shout he fell into the water on his back, and Hugh and Christopher went with him.

XIX

Victory

'VICTORY,' said the goblin. 'We win.'

'Down with giants,' said the ravens, and walked like aldermen to watch the watery struggles.

The goblin and the alchemist came into the water to bring out Hugh and Christopher. But the giant had not finished with them yet. With his last struggles he pulled both rescuers under, and then, defeated, he let them both go and floated on his back, kicking a little with his heels.

The goblin stood up, and they all stood with him with water falling off them. The giant was slowly moving out into the Mere, like a drifting log.

'Hold him,' said the goblin, 'he's swimming with his feet. It's no good if he gets away.'

'Can we touch him now?' said Christopher.

'Quite safe,' said the goblin. 'Just push him back here, and the ravens can look after him.'

The giant whimpered, and blew up a fountain of water.

'You've lost,' said the goblin. 'Do you give in, or shall we drown you?'

'I surrender,' said the giant. 'Eleven to one: not fair.'

'You had a bicycle,' said the goblin. 'And you should have complained before we began, and you could have had single combat with the bear.'

The giant shuddered, and the water rippled away from him.

The goblin ordered the ravens on to the giant, and they stood on him as if he were a raft, and looked at the water suspiciously.

'What we want,' said the alchemist, 'and I wish I had thought to bring it, is my new Mop-it-up household and pioneering duster, guaranteed to hold five gallons of any liquid. Only two hours each. Can be wrung out and used half a dozen times.'

'You've never brought us anything at all,' said Hugh. 'But you did fight quite well.'

'I'm not valiant,' said the alchemist. 'I invent things that don't need a valiant heart behind them; then I forget to bring them.'

'Never mind about all that,' said the goblin. 'We've got business to see to.'

'With me, I suppose,' said the giant. 'Do you mind telling your jackdaws not to look at my tongue like that.'

'Put up with it,' said Christopher. 'You're not entitled to any consideration in your state.'

'Well said,' said the goblin.

'They say it to me at school,' said Christopher. 'I've never been able to say it to anybody.'

The goblin spoke to the giant again. 'Stop swimming with your feet,' he said. 'Or I'll tie you up like a boat. We must settle with you first of all, and then get dry.'

'What do you want to do with me?' said the giant. 'Do anything you like, but don't let me go: I could never bear the disgrace of being free after losing a small battle like that.'

'Don't believe him,' said the goblin. 'He's only pretending he'd hate it most. No, what we want from you, giant, is a promise to sell this battlefield to these young Princes or their father, to build a palace on.'

'I don't want to,' said the giant.

'And you will also sell them the island on the Mere.'

'I couldn't,' said the giant. 'The shame is too much for me. I'm going to drown myself.'

'You haven't the strength,' said the goblin. 'My friend the alchemist will write out an agreement for you to sign.'

The alchemist was sitting on the ground, with water dripping from his hair on to his hands, and seemed not to be listening.

'I'll do it if he'll let me have a peacock,' he said. 'I've always fancied a peacock. If I don't do it then he can't sign it and we'll have to leave him in the water.'

'Take anything you like,' said the giant, his voice growing fainter and fainter.

'Here it is,' said the alchemist. He screwed up his face, and began to mutter to himself. Then he pulled out of his pocket a piece of parchment already covered with writing, and from another pocket brought out a feather and a bottle of ink.

'Indestructible Alchemist's Black,' he said. 'Made from soot out of my own chimney, and a few other things. Come up, giant, and sign this magically written treaty.'

'What does it say?' said the giant, in a whisper.

' "Whereas I am truly defeated in battle by the most valiant princes Christopher and Hugh and their worthy and unworthy" (me) "friends, I do offer in token of my defeat to the said princes that open land whereon I was defeated and routed to be theirs for ever and likewise I deliver to them the island next across the water to be theirs for ever and I do guarantee them peace from my own ravages for ever all this do I agree to and sign to without any force being exerted upon me and of my own free will".'

'It's not my own free will,' said the giant.

'I'm not responsible for the writing,' said the alchemist. 'I ground down some solicitors into that ink and they wrote it.'

'By magic,' said Hugh. 'Come up and sign it.'

'But,' said the giant, piping in a thin voice. 'But . . .'

'What now,' said the goblin.

'Only that,' said the giant. 'Only that I can't.'

'Why?' said Christopher. 'You've been beaten: you must obey the rule.'

'I can't write,' said the giant, and sank.

The ravens flew up as the water touched their feet.

Hugh and Christopher ran into the water and pulled the giant ashore, and lifted his head from the water. He blew out more Mere and shook his head gently. 'I'm finished,' he said. 'Disgraced, illiterate, damp, weak, defeated.'

'You can sign with a cross,' said the alchemist. 'That's always done in the best circles. What we really need is my Self-Educator on Greek Principles, in three leather-bound volumes, one year each, containing the fundamentals of every branch of learning, except, of course, reading, which you have to know already.'

'Then it wouldn't be any good to him,' said Christopher.

'He could look at the pictures,' said the alchemist. 'Not that there are any, though. Never mind. Sit him up, and if he can scrawl with a cross I'll witness it: no fee.'

Hugh and Christopher lifted the giant up, put the wet parchment on his own knee, which was just above water, put the pen in his hand, put the ink bottle to it, and told him to put a cross at the bottom of the paper.

'Like a kiss,' said Hugh. 'You know.'

The giant put the inky end of the quill pen on the paper and made a sprawly cross that began to run into the wet on the parchment. The alchemist snatched the parchment away and dried it by spreading sand on it from an un-splashed place on the little beach.

'Now,' said the goblin, 'that's done.'

'Nearly,' said the alchemist, and took the pen from the giant and signed his own name, which was unreadable, and wrote under it that he was the witness to the signature of 'the giant living by the Mere'.

'It's done now,' he said. 'Your agreement, your Highnesses, signed and wetnessed, I mean, witnessed.'

Christopher took it, being the eldest.

'Good heavens,' said the goblin. 'Your watch: it's been in the water.'

'It's all right,' said Christopher. 'It's a swimming watch, and it doesn't mind.'

'I took mine off,' said the goblin, and he said to one of the ravens 'Dolly, my watch is on the peg.' The raven flew away over the wood, and the others watched enviously.

'Now we'll go and look at the water on the island,' said the goblin. 'Giant, you can come too. Get up, and we'll walk there. It's not very deep, you see,' he told Hugh and Christopher. 'I think you found that out on your first journey.'

'We had to go a long way round to get there,' said Christopher. 'But that was from the other side.'

'We'll go from this side,' said the goblin. 'We're wet already. You're not cold, are you?'

'Not at all,' said Hugh.

'You will be soon,' said goblin. 'But we'll get you back before then: the island's on the way.'

They walked to the island from the place where they had first seen the giant standing, when he threw stones at them. The giant walked in the water all the way, with Hugh keeping a wary eye on him, because he seemed so much recovered in strength.

The water was waist deep at its worst, and the greater

part of the journey was no more than knee deep. Hugh looked for crayfish, but there were none.

They were halfway there when the raven came back with the goblin's watch, circled in the air to deliver it, and then landed on the goblin's shoulder.

'I think we ought to have the bear,' said the alchemist, and went to get it. The goblin whistled for the other ravens, and they flew overhead for escort. The alchemist caught them up at the island with the bear swimming and paddling behind him, off the chain altogether.

'Now,' said the goblin. 'Just move that hill away, will you, giant?'

'Certainly,' said the giant. He shook himself, and then turned his strength, which had come back on reaching dry land, to tearing the top of the hill away. The turf came away in lumps, only root deep, and below there was a flat slab of stone. When the slab was clear all round the giant lifted it, and straightaway there gushed out a lop-sided fountain all among the ravens, who slipped down the wind out of the way.

'Plenty of water,' said the alchemist. 'Is this the precious fluid I tested in my workshop?'

'The very same,' said the goblin. 'This, giant, is what will flow in the palace of these princes.'

'If I may be allowed to taste it occasionally,' said the giant, 'on Wednesdays, perhaps, I will be the palace's most devoted servant. I might even help to build it, if it isn't done by magic means overnight, suddenly.'

'I dare say it will be,' said the alchemist. 'I have a nice little thing in that line, at present only for making shelter for the night, for travellers, and not very expensive: a day a pinch. I dare say I could make up a larger quantity with real windows.'

'We must go back for tea,' said Christopher. 'She told us not to be late.'

'Put the stone back,' said the goblin. 'I think we'd better go back with you, and explain to Mrs Wrigley about the game. We didn't really intend you to get wet, did we, John?'

'I couldn't resist it in the end,' said the giant. 'I'll come along and explain everything.'

'But I'm afraid,' said the goblin, 'that Mrs Wrigley has a low opinion of us altogether. Mr Wrigley is, after all, a respectable man, and we are only, what, John?'

'Circus folk,' said the giant. 'Pantomime players, jugglers in fairgrounds.'

'Well, we mustn't stand here and talk,' said the alchemist. 'We'd better hurry up and meet Mrs Wrigley and get it over. But I'm afraid we shan't see you again. I don't know why we've seen you so often already.'

'She thinks we're on the beach,' said Hugh.

They left the island behind, when the giant had dropped the stone again and sealed away the fountain. The ravens came back overhead, and the bear walked damply among them like a dog.

'I hope you aren't going to get into trouble,' said the goblin. 'You must blame us as much as you can.'

XX

Departure

'OUR real names are these,' said the giant. 'I am John March, and the alchemist here is my cousin Peter, who teaches teachers how to teach. He's having a holiday with me now, before I go travelling for the summer with the circus. Your friend the goblin—my friend too—is Howard Gray, and his aim in life is to have a flying chariot pulled by his ravens. I could have had a share in my father's business, which makes a great deal of furniture in London; but instead of the share in the work I took money, because business didn't interest me. But the money gets worth less and less. Never mind. And I go with the circus because we don't laugh at each other there, whether we're dwarf or giant. It's very difficult to be an ordinary person if you're a dwarf or a giant. Circus life is right for us: they like to have us around because we're of unusual size. Howard always wanted to be a doctor, like his grandfather.'

'But it didn't seem right,' said the goblin. 'Not when I'm so small. People would think it odd. It's not very hard to be laughed at.'

'But a different matter if you're trying to be laughed at in the circus ring,' said the giant.

'You get used to it, I suppose,' said Christopher.

'Yes,' said the giant. 'And it's all right in the end.'

'But a lot of people think we're a kind of gipsy, robbing hen-roosts and putting out birds' eyes and all sorts of imaginary things,' said the goblin. 'Mrs Wrigley's one of them. That's the worst of being respectable: you've always got to have someone in mind to be better than, and she's busy being better than us.'

They reached the edge of the lake and came up out of the water for the last time, and into the wood.

'I don't know whether you'll be able to get through the hole in the hedge, giant,' said Hugh. 'The goblin can, and so can we.'

'We'll drag him through,' said the goblin. But in the end he stood on the top of the cliff and stepped over, and they all went down the field called Egypt to the road, the giant, the goblin, the alchemist, the bear, two boys and six ravens.

When they came to where they could see the house they saw a car in front of it.

'She's got visitors as well,' said Christopher. 'And I'm getting cold.'

'It isn't visitors,' said Hugh, watching somebody putting a suitcase into the car. 'It's them. Mother and Dad.'

'Oh, that'll be all right,' said Christopher. 'Come on, giant, they won't mind you.'

'Perhaps . . .' said the giant.

'We'll have to explain, John,' said the goblin.

Hugh and Christopher ran ahead.

'Well I never,' said Mrs Wrigley. 'What have you been doing? Have you been in the sea?'

Neither of them bothered with Mrs Wrigley. Mother and Dad did not mind a hug as wet as a mermaid's; and they hugged first and asked questions afterwards.

'You're both shivering,' said Mother. 'Did you fall in the sea?'

'No,' said Christopher. 'There's a lake over there called the Mere, and there's a lovely place to build a house. We had to fight the giant about it this afternoon.'

'How long have you been playing there?' said Mrs Wrigley.

Dad put Hugh down when he felt his dampness soaking through. 'I thought it was a circus approaching,' he said. 'All those vultures, or what have you.'

'It is a circus,' said Christopher. 'But they're very nice, and they fight if you want; and we've been with them all the time. The goblin lent us a boat.'

'There's altogether too much shivering,' said Mother. 'I think you ought to have a bath, and then we'll be on our way.'

'Are you going?' said Christopher. 'Why didn't you say you were coming?'

'We did,' said Mother. 'Mrs Wrigley must have kept it as a surprise for you.'

'They didn't want to be round the house all day,' said Mrs Wrigley.

'No,' said Hugh. 'Never.'

'We aren't going without you,' said Mother. 'Is there some hot water, Maud?'

'There's plenty,' said Mrs Wrigley. 'We'll put them in at once, and you'll have to take those cases out of the car and change all their clothes. I hope you don't think I encourage them to behave like this?' That remark was meant mostly for the giant and the goblin and the alchemist. Christopher considered that he and Hugh would hardly have been alive if Mother and Dad hadn't been there to save them from Mrs Wrigley's anger.

Mother took them both upstairs, and Dad stayed outside to talk with the giant and the other two. The ravens sat on the gate and looked at the black cat. The bear climbed into the car and went to sleep. The goblin had to pull it out when Mother came for cases with the dry clothes in.

When the bath was over, including a very long explanation to Mother of all that had happened, and a combined opinion of Mrs Wrigley ('we came as soon as we could,' said Mother. 'We knew she was pretty dull.'), and they all came down, the giant, the goblin and the alchemist had gone, but the ravens were still there, and the bear was in the car, not really asleep but pretending to be.

'I don't know anything about those people,' said Mrs Wrigley. 'Wrigley and I don't associate with them.'

'They told us all about it,' said Christopher. 'But they're the nicest people we've met.'

'Good sorts,' said Dad. 'Nervous, though, of being looked at off duty, so to speak. Wanted to know about prospects in Africa. Interesting.'

'Did they tell you about our land?' said Christopher, and he handed over the document signed by the giant. 'I think he can write, really.'

'He can,' said Dad. 'Knows about the Stock Exchange. Wealthy man, I gather, once, but money isn't what it was.'

'Did he tell you about our land?' said Hugh. 'We won.'

'Said something about it,' said Dad. 'But I don't want to settle down yet: not too old to see the world, I said. Back to Africa in a couple of months.'

'Us as well?' said Christopher, hoping it would be yes.

'See about it,' said Dad. 'School to consider; but we're on holiday now.'

That meant no. 'See about it' always did.

'You won't be alone any more,' said Mother. 'Hugh will be with you.'

'And can we stay with the giant for our holidays?' said Hugh. 'Christopher says school's like . . .' But he thought he had better not say any more in front of Mrs Wrigley.

'Those circus people have returned,' said Mrs Wrigley, to change the course of the conversation.

'Good,' said Dad. 'Enterprising people, I think. Can we invite them in for a cup of char, eh, Maud?'

'Wrigley would not like it,' said Mrs Wrigley. 'Even if I did. Will you tell them to remove their rooks?'

Hugh and Christopher went outside to say good-bye.

'She won't have anything to do with you,' said Hugh.

'We know,' said the giant. 'Your parents didn't mind, though.'

'No,' said Christopher. 'But they don't want to build a house, so our fight was wasted.'

'Not at all,' said the giant. 'Not the slightest bit. If you ever come here again, that battlefield is yours to do what you like with. Perhaps your father will settle down in time and come here to live.'

'We had a jolly good time,' said Hugh. 'Even when we were frightened. I shall always think I'm a prince.'

'It's a very good thought,' said the goblin. 'I shall always think I'm a goblin, and then I shan't mind so much only being a dwarf.'

'I can't say I shall study alchemy,' said the alchemist, 'but I've enjoyed my holiday a great deal; and so has my cousin John here, and his friend Howard. I wish all my

pupils were as sensible about what they see as you two
have been.'

'It was the best time I've ever had,' said Christopher.
'And with Mother home as well it's even better.'

Dad came out to the car with the repacked suitcases. The
goblin dragged the bear out of the car and made him sit on
the lawn, in spite of Mrs Wrigley's look through the
window.

'I'm grateful to you three,' said Dad. 'I'm not anxious
about Chris if he's at school; but with the two of them
we had to send them to Maud; and she hasn't much idea.
We'd've left them longer if we'd known they were so
happy.'

'I think they've enjoyed themselves,' said the goblin.
'We gave them something to do.'

'Dad, come and see where we were,' said Christopher.
'You could see the place you could build a house on.'

'Haven't time, old man,' said Dad. 'We've a fair distance
to go. Hop in and say good-bye and thank you to Mrs
Wrigley.'

'Going now?' said Christopher.

'Five minutes,' said Dad. 'Hurry up.'

'We will,' said Hugh. They both went in, and said good-
bye in a quick way to Mrs Wrigley. Hugh ran upstairs
and got his bag of sand, that Mother had taken out of the
case. He brought it so that their deceit should not be found
out. They said good-bye to the black cat, which was
sheltering in the kitchen away from the ravens. They said
good-bye to the bear, who looked in their pockets and

said good-bye back, shaking hands when the goblin told
him to.

The ravens said 'Good-bye' in their coky voices, and
added 'Down with giants' and 'I want my breakfast' until
the goblin told them to stop.

Then Mother was in the car, the giant's hands and the
goblin's and the alchemist's were shaken, the car started,
and they went.

'Come on, my children,' said the goblin, and the ravens
flew above them and the bear followed behind, and the
three friends walked away in silence.